YORK NOTES

General Editors: Professor A.N. Jeffares (*University of Stirling*) & Professor Suheil Bushrui (*American University of Beirut*)

D.H. Lawrence

WOMEN IN LOVE

Notes by Neil McEwan

MA B LITT (OXFORD) PH D (STIRLING)
Lecturer in English, University of Qatar

LONGMAN
YORK PRESS

YORK PRESS
Immeuble Esseily, Place Riad Solh, Beirut

LONGMAN GROUP LIMITED
Longman House, Burnt Mill, Harlow,
Essex CM20 2JE, England
Associated companies, branches and representatives
throughout the world

First published 1981
Eighth impression 1995

ISBN 0-582-04034-5

Produced by Longman Singapore Publishers Pte Ltd
Printed in Singapore

Contents

Part 1

Introduction

The author's life

David Herbert Richards Lawrence was born at Eastwood, a colliery town in the Nottinghamshire countryside, in 1885. His father was a coal-miner, uneducated but a good story-teller, a dancer and nature-lover, and a man of energy and warmth. His mother, a former teacher, had married for love but soon came to resent her husband's coarseness. The five children grew up in a divided, often violent home. David Herbert (the fourth child) was impressed by his father's stories of the mines, but was closer to his mother, especially in adolescence after she nursed him through an illness. *Sons and Lovers* (1913), Lawrence's third novel, portrays, in the hero's love for his mother and her inhibiting possessiveness, the author's own experience.

He owed much to Mrs Lawrence's ambition for her children. Regular attendance at chapel and Sunday-school gave him a thorough knowledge of the Bible, whose style and imagery influenced all his later writing. The chapel's Protestant, Nonconformist tradition helped to form Lawrence's blend of moral seriousness and unconventionality, and—as he recognised—a tendency to preach. At twelve, urged on by his mother, he won a scholarship to Nottingham High School. He became a pupil-teacher in 1902, and, after two years (1906-8) at Nottingham University College, a schoolmaster in Croydon.

He read widely during these years and discussed what he read with friends, including Jessie Chambers, a friend from a farm near his home; she encouraged him and helped with his earliest stories and poems. He lost his faith in Christianity and began to develop his own religion—venerating 'all gods' and the 'true nature' of Man; it was to inspire his whole life and work. His first novel, *The White Peacock*, came out in 1911, full of faults, yet impressive—and, Lawrence said, 'all about love'.

In 1912 he met the wife of a Nottingham professor; she left her husband and children for Lawrence and they married in 1914. Frieda came from an aristocratic German family (the von Richthofens). Their marriage was troubled but secure. After the appearance of *Sons and Lovers*, Lawrence found recognition and friends in literary London. Ford Madox Ford (formerly Ford Madox Hueffer, 1873-1939), who published Lawrence's earliest pieces in his monthly *The English Review*, had already announced him as a 'big genius'. By 1914, having given up teaching because of illness, Lawrence was a professional writer.

The outbreak of war, which almost demoralised him, brought practical problems: he returned from Germany (where he had been living with Frieda) and moved through various parts of England, unfit for military service, but suspected by the police, partly because his wife was German. He hoped to go to America to found a new type of community—a project called 'Rananim' which interested him all his life; but in 1917 he was refused a passport.

He planned a novel which would be more original, in method and approach to character, than his previous work. Provisionally called 'The Sisters', this became *The Rainbow* (published in 1915) and *Women in Love* (written in 1916). The first edition of *The Rainbow*, considered obscene by most reviewers, was destroyed by court-order. Undeterred, Lawrence wrote and rewrote *Women in Love*, using characters and settings from *The Rainbow* but producing a novel complete in itself and not a sequel in the usual sense. The first English edition was brought out, despite attempts to suppress it, in 1921.

After the war the Lawrences travelled abroad, moving from Florence and Sicily to Ceylon, Australia, and New Mexico; he died of tuberculosis in France in 1930.

His later books continued to study relations between the sexes (with a boldness that often offended). The best later novels are *The Plumed Serpent* (1926) and *Lady Chatterley's Lover*, which was not published unexpurgated in England until 1960. *Kangaroo* (1923) is concerned with social and political problems. Lawrence thought *Women in Love* his best novel, and so do many readers. His output was prolific: he published over fifty books—poems, short stories, essays, travel books, and polemic. He was a painter with a flair for colour, an able teacher, a talker, and a keen observer. He was intrigued and inspired by exotic and ancient cultures (Aztec and Etruscan), though his imagination was dominated by the English Midland scenes of his early life.

Lawrence could be infuriating in his dogmatism and combativeness; but his energy and charm, humour and courage were always attractive. He could be naive (as he was in dismissing most philosophy and science) in advancing his own creed of 'the blood', 'the dark gods', and 'the man alive'; he was at his best a visionary, but at worst tedious. Lawrence has divided critical opinion, finding impassioned disciples and detractors. He believed in his own talents and was dedicated to the full use of them. He made himself a part of modern culture.

General background

The Rainbow traces the industrial transformation of a rural community in the course of the nineteenth century; the earlier novel helps to explain the background to *Women in Love*. For generations the Brangwens have lived close to the land they work as farmers; in early Victorian days, squire and vicar were figures of absolute authority in a country village. The coming of railways and mines brings new kinds of hardship and ugliness to the Brangwens' world. (Lawrence considered the worst offence of the Victorian industrialists that of forcing ugliness on the lives of ordinary people.) It also extends the possibilities of life: Ursula leaves home to become a teacher. Her independence and knowledge of life, before marriage, would have been incomprehensible to earlier generations of Brangwens.

Lawrence hated the effects of English industrial and urban growth. He loathed vulgarity in all social classes, and the materialism and conventionality which he thought had enfeebled 'the tough old England that made us'. In *Women in Love* he attacked—in Gerald and his father—two generations of colliery-owners who had lost touch with life. He also ridiculed modernist intellectuals, such as Hermione Roddice and Halliday in the novel. These characters are familiar with radical ideas: with the theory of evolution in the *Origin of Species* (1859) by Charles Darwin (1809–82), with the psychology of Sigmund Freud (1856–1939), and with the philosophy of Friedrich Nietzsche (1844–1900)—anti-Christian and 'Dionysian', supporting the 'animal instincts' of Man against 'Apollonian' rationalism. Lawrence, like Birkin in *Women in Love*, was influenced by these writers. But just as Birkin attacks Hermione for shallow intellectualism, Lawrence despised all ideologies and systems which led people away from morality as he understood it: truth to one's own manhood or womanhood. What that meant took Lawrence—like Birkin—time and confusion of mind to work out. But from the start of his career he was dissatisfied not only with modern social conditions but also with much of modern thought.

Socialism was one creed popular among intellectuals and Lawrence was infatuated with it for a time. In 1915 he wrote to the philosopher Bertrand Russell (1872–1970) that the framework of society must be 'smashed' and everything nationalised. (The Russian Revolution was about to begin when he was writing *Women in Love*.) But he quickly became impatient with socialism. The First World War disillusioned him. 'In 1915 the old world ended', he wrote later in *Kangaroo*. Mankind had fallen into a shameful hatred, he felt; belief in progress was discredited. Birkin's pessimism about human destiny reflects Lawrence's own doubts. Birkin's ideas, like the author's, are more concerned with how to live than with how to organise society. Lawrence's life and work were shaped by these historical developments. Although it had always been possible for an able young man to free himself through writing from a background of poverty, it was easier for Lawrence, after the 1870 Education Act and the advance of free schooling, to escape from a life of trivial labour. The gradual 'breaking down of social barriers' referred to in *Women in Love* allowed him to move relatively easily through English society, as do Ursula and Gudrun in the novel. Their freedom to choose jobs, friends and styles of life was not achieved by most English girls until later in the century.

In some ways Lawrence was fortunate in living when he did. He had troubles with censors but he managed to publish most of his work and to find a readership. Travel—except during the war—was relatively easy. He lived in circles where freedom of thought was taken for granted. It was unfortunate, however, that he reached his maturity as a writer during the First World War when English public opinion was at its most narrow-minded.

'His problems were central to a main current of growth and difficulty in our society and our culture', writes Raymond Williams.* The emancipation of women, the effects of industrialism, education in a democratic society, personal freedom in a modern state—issues which the characters face in *Women in Love*—are still growing problems, and not only in English society. Lawrence is more widely read today than ever before.

Literary background

Lawrence's critical writings show a broad knowledge of English, French, German, Russian and American literature, and also an impatience with almost all earlier novelists. Because he learned from so many other writers and because he was determined to obey his own instincts as a writer and not produce 'imitations' of other people's books, it is difficult to point to precise influences. As a young teacher, Lawrence admired *Anna Karenina* (1875-6) by the Russian writer Leo Tolstoy (1828-1910) more than any other novel, but he later spoke slightingly of Tolstoy and of another Russian novelist, Feodor Dostoevsky (1821-81), whom he thought morbid. *Buddenbrooks* (1901) by the German Thomas Mann (1875-1955) may have inspired 'The Sisters', but Lawrence attacked Mann's preoccupation with formal beauty,

The English Novel from Dickens to Lawrence, Chatto & Windus, 1970, Chapter 8.

a 'complaint' which he attributed to the French novelist Gustave Flaubert (1821–80). He is clearly indebted to these European writers, and to English novelists from Jane Austen (1775–1817) to Henry James (1843–1916)—both of whom he disparaged at times. Some critics maintain that his strong moral sense derives from the English tradition in fiction; others that his awareness of social relations was acquired from English novels. It was necessary, though, for Lawrence to disown traditions in order to clarify what he wanted to write.

Many nineteenth-century English novelists, with a large public to entertain, relied on complicated plots, melodrama and sentiment; they were carefully reticent about sexual relations. These conventions were accepted by the most serious and imaginative writers. The master of such popular fiction was Charles Dickens (1812–70), whom Lawrence sometimes recalls in his power to create minor characters. Lawrence called these conventions 'childish', although he recognised their power; he saw too that he could not excel the Victorians as a story-teller. Towards the end of the century Henry James, following French and Russian models, brought an artistry to the English novel which Lawrence suspected: the danger was of putting art before life (as the sculptor Loerke does in *Women in Love*). James would, justifiably, have denied that; but Lawrence, who claimed to be bored by plots like Dickens's, also wanted to avoid James's contrived elegance.

George Eliot (Mary Ann Evans, 1819–80) and Thomas Hardy (1840–1928) are the English novelists with whom he has most in common. Both came from the provinces; both made themselves familiar with European culture; both put intellectual discussions into their stories. They shared a love of nature and a sympathy with uneducated people; they could see historical processes in English life, and show private acts against a social and universal background. Lawrence resembles them in these respects; but, in reading him, there is no sense of imitation.

Lawrence was not alone among his contemporaries in wanting to make a fresh start in fiction. He admired (with reservations) Joseph Conrad (1857–1924), and he read Marcel Proust (1871–1922) and James Joyce (1882–1941)—both more radical in technical innovation than Lawrence himself. But he kept apart from literary movements. When *Sons and Lovers* brought success, he came to know Katherine Mansfield (1888–1923), John Middleton Murry (1889–1957), E.M. Forster (1879–1970), and other literary figures, some of whom he portrayed unflatteringly in *Women in Love*. He remained his own man.

English poetry is part of the literary background to the novels. His characters are readers of poetry. John Keats (1795–1821), P.B. Shelley (1792–1822), S.T. Coleridge (1772–1834), and Robert Browning (1812–

89), are quoted in *Women in Love*. Imagery, mood and rhythm show the author's familiarity with Romantic poetry. Lawrence's own verse improved when he discovered the American Walt Whitman (1819-92). He wrote only a few entirely successful poems, but his imagination was that of a poet.

A note on the text

Women in Love was written between April and November, 1916. It was privately printed in New York in 1920 and published in London in 1921 by Martin Secker. There is an edition by William Heinemann, London, 1954. A paperback edition was issued by Penguin Books, Harmondsworth, in 1960; this has been constantly reprinted. Page references in these Notes are to the Penguin edition.

Part 2

Summaries
of WOMEN IN LOVE

A general summary

Ursula and Gudrun Brangwen are dissatisfied with their lives at home as unmarried schoolteachers in a small mining town in the Midlands of England. At a wedding in the neighbourhood, each notices a young man. Ursula is intrigued by Rupert Birkin, a school-inspector. She has met him briefly and would like to know him better. Gudrun is attracted by Gerald Crich, the handsome, hard-working son of the local colliery-owner.

Birkin is under the sway of his mistress, Hermione Roddice, a baronet's daughter, a woman of strong will and advanced opinions. With Birkin she visits Ursula's school and invites the sisters to the country house—Breadalby—which she shares with her brother. At the house-party Birkin becomes interested in Ursula. His relationship with Hermione has become highly strained and quarrelsome. Overwrought, Hermione strikes him with a paperweight, and he escapes from her demanding dependence on him. Gerald Crich, who is tiring of the kind of girl he can pay for during trips to London, is attracted by Gudrun. He thinks of her as a social inferior, but she is beautiful, unusual—and an artist.

Birkin is filled with a despairing contempt for the modern industrial-ised world in which his friend Gerald has flourished by bringing new technology to the mines. Birkin believes in spontaneity, sensuality, and society's need for a fresh start; he has little hope for mankind, but retains a private faith in 'ultimate' marriage and ideal friendship. He elaborates his views with Gerald and with Ursula. She finds his 'preach-ing' tiresome; a feminine grasp of reality tells her that much of his talk about humanity's doom is wrong; but she likes him. Though frail and sickly, he has energy, liveliness and integrity.

Gudrun is fascinated by Gerald. When the sisters watch him forcing his mare (terrified by the noise of a passing train) to stand at a railway-crossing, Ursula is horrified at his cruelty. Gudrun is excited.

Ursula is jealous of Hermione, who is trying to recover her power over Birkin. Birkin abandons his belief in sensuality and develops a theory of marriage as a union beyond love in which the partners are like two stars in harmony: independent, but committed to each other. He wants to combine such a relationship with an ideal friendship with Gerald. Ursula simply wants him to love her. He fears the 'Great Mother' instinct of a woman which makes her want to dominate a man.

The two relationships intensify and the contrast between them becomes clearer during a lake-party given by old Mr Crich at Shortlands, the family home. Birkin is still beset by problems—intellectual, sexual and spiritual—while Ursula hopes for uncomplicated happiness; but their partnership comes to seem healthier and more promising than that of Gerald and Gudrun which increasingly appears limited, perverse, and perhaps even deadly.

The lake-party ends with the drowning of Gerald's sister and her would-be rescuer. (Gerald, ominously, killed his brother in a childhood accident.) Mr Crich is dying. Frequent mention of death creates a sombre background to the courtship. An incident in which Gerald ruthlessly subdues a boisterous pet rabbit (belonging to the youngest Crich child, Winifred, who is now Gudrun's pupil) implies that a pleasure in cruelty and wilfulness is a part of the bond between them.

Birkin is trying to accept the prospect of marriage. One night he throws stones into the moon's reflection in a pool, seeing there the power of ancient goddesses and the dominating urge which he fears in women. Another evening he wrestles naked with Gerald, pursuing inward health through bodily contact. He emerges more stable from these encounters. After difficulties and quarrels, he and Ursula become lovers, resign from their jobs, and agree to marry when Ursula is ready. Their first night together, spent out in the forest, leaves them mystically united. Ursula delays the marriage, however, until she is 'ready in herself'; then quarrels with her parents when he announces it too abruptly. The marriage takes place and Birkin, who now believes that Ursula has saved him from the desperate confusion of his past life, insists that she write to her parents.

Mr Crich dies. A few nights later Gerald visits his father's grave and then makes his way to Gudrun's bedroom. Although he is comforted and reassured after their night together, Gudrun is not. There is no mystic union here. When Birkin renews his offer of sacred friendship it is implied that Gerald, in refusing, shows himself too inhibited to make the restless Gudrun happy as a wife.

The two couples (Gerald and Gudrun not yet married) spend a Christmas holiday in Austria. Departure from England brings Ursula and Birkin closer, but Gudrun is unable to return Gerald's passion. When the Birkins go south to Italy, Gundrun decides that she will not marry Gerald and they become trapped in a dreadful conflict. She flirts with another guest at the hostel—a gnome-like sculptor—until Gerald, in a rage, attempts to kill her. He then walks to his death in the mountains. Gudrun is unmoved. Birkin regrets the friendship, and with it the completeness of life that he might have known.

Detailed summaries

Chapter 1. Sisters

Ursula Brangwen, at twenty-six, and her sister Gudrun, at twenty-five, are unmarried and living at home, teaching at a grammar school. Gudrun, who has been an art student in London, observes that marriage is the next step. Both are nervous of the subject. They set out to see a wedding taking place at Willey Green near their Midland mining town of Beldover.

Smartly dressed (Gudrun likes brightly-coloured stockings), they appear out of place on their walk; Gudrun hates the way the mines spoil the countryside. At the wedding, Gudrun is attracted by the bride's brother, Gerald Crich, the son of the colliery-owner. Handsome and successful, he looks an upright English gentleman. Ursula wonders about Rupert Birkin, whom she knows slightly as a school-inspector. Slight and pale and unconventional, he hides his awkwardness; she is irritated and charmed by him. She watches, too, the striking, aristocratic figure of Hermione Roddice, a remarkable woman and an intellectual of radical views. Beneath her imposing public figure Hermione feels vulnerable; she depends on her relationship with Birkin and dreads losing him.

There is a cheer from the crowd when the bridegroom arrives late and chases after the bride. The girls' father, Will Brangwen, a school handicraft instructor, plays the wedding march. When the guests leave the church Hermione possessively seeks out Birkin. Gudrun is deeply disturbed by the sight of Gerald Crich.

NOTES AND GLOSSARY:

Artemis:	Greek goddess of hunting and chastity
Hebe:	Greek goddess of youth and cupbearer to the gods
reculer pour mieux sauter:	(*French*) stepping back in order to jump further ahead
Chelsea:	a district of south-west London which is frequented by artists
Sussex:	a pleasant, rural county in the south of England, quite different from Beldover

Chapter 2. Shortlands

The Criches' home, 'a sort of manor farm', is in the country but within sight of smoke from the mines. Gerald is host after the wedding because his father is ill. Skirts rustle and servants hurry. Birkin and the eccentric Mrs Crich talk about people: people don't matter, Birkin says. She speaks enigmatically about her children (she has many). Gerald is really the weakest, although he seems strong. She would like him to have a friend.

During lunch the talk becomes general and theoretical. Hermione and Birkin are opposed to 'a spirit of emulation' in society; Gerald thinks it a spur to productivity and progress. After the meal Birkin and Gerald discuss the bride's conduct in racing with the groom at the church this morning. Birkin defends spontaneous individuality. He accuses the conventional Gerald of cynicism, based on unhappiness. There is a tension between the two men, who are attracted despite their differences.

NOTES AND GLOSSARY:

Cain: he killed his brother and was cursed (see the Bible, Genesis 4:8–16)

Gerald as a boy: this is based on a real accident in similar circumstances, at a colliery-owner's house near Eastwood

Chapter 3. Class-room

Birkin visits Ursula at school while she is giving a nature lesson on hazel catkins. As they examine the flowers (he wants the children to colour the red stigmas and yellow catkins in their sketch-books), Ursula begins to feel the excitement of love and Birkin looks at her 'with a new pleasure'.

Hermione now intrudes, having spotted Birkin's car. They discuss the reproduction of flowers, and Hermione (who admires the small wood-carvings that Gudrun specialises in) invites the sisters to stay at Breadalby, her father's country-house. Ursula is wary of Hermione, surprised by her bullying and yet intimate manner.

Birkin is furious with Hermione when (misinterpreting his own views) she suggests that education develops consciousness at the expense of spontaneity. Her claim to value 'animal instincts', he tells her, is only a form of intellectualism. He accuses her of a lust for power. Ursula, listening, is frightened by the hatred between them. Birkin tells Ursula that sensuality is all he values now as a key to living. She senses a 'richness and liberty' in him, and when he leaves she weeps without knowing why.

NOTES AND GLOSSARY:

Lady of Shalott: she sees the world through a mirror in the poem of this title (1852) by Alfred, Lord Tennyson (1809–92)

pythoness: the priestess of Apollo (who slew a python) at the oracle of Delphi in ancient Greece was called the Pythia

woman wailing for her demon lover: a line from the poem 'Kubla Khan' (1797) by Samuel Taylor Coleridge (1772–1834)

Chapter 4. Diver

The next Saturday Ursula and Gudrun walk to Willey Water, the lake at Shortlands. As they reach the boathouse Gerald dives and they watch him swimming. Gudrun envies him, and envies men their freedom to do as they please. This leads to discussion of Gerald's improvements at the mines and the accident in which he killed his brother. Gerald will have to die soon, Ursula says facetiously, when there is nothing left to improve. They meet Hermione and Laura Crich. Ursula thinks Hermione rude. Gudrun admires her freedom from snobbishness in asking teachers—social inferiors—to stay with her. The sisters argue about what really constitutes smart behaviour. Ursula calls herself a swan among geese: she puts up with her weekly duties at school, but hopes for something better soon.

NOTES AND GLOSSARY:

a Nibelung: a creature of ancient Germanic legend

Dorothy Wordsworth: the poet William Wordsworth's sister and companion (1771–1855)

pour moi elle n'existe pas: (*French*) for me she does not exist

à terre: (*French*) *terre à terre* means pedestrian, down to earth

Corneille: Pierre Corneille (1606–84) French dramatist, whose characters make grand, pompous speeches

je m'en fiche: (*French*) I don't care

Chapter 5. In the train

Birkin and Gerald meet on a railway platform, waiting for the London train, and travel together. An article in Gerald's newspaper argues that the country will soon be ruined unless new values can be found. Birkin does not believe that people are willing to break up existing society to create a new world. Industrialised England has become dreary and inert with materialism. Gerald lives for his work, he says, and for 'making things *go*'. Birkin's ambition is private: his ideal is an 'ultimate marriage'.

Gerald is unimpressed. He likes Birkin but does not take him seriously; Birkin knows and resents it. He says how much he dislikes the minor artists—and their girls—whom he knows in London. When Gerald shows an interest in the girls, Birkin suggests that they meet again that night at an artists' café, the Pompadour. Entering London, he feels 'like one of the damned'.

NOTES AND GLOSSARY:

Sodom: an ancient, corrupt city destroyed by divine justice (see Genesis 13, 18, 19)

Pompadour: the café is named after the Marquise de Pompadour (1721-64), mistress of the French King Louis XV. She patronised literature and the arts

'where the quiet-coloured end of evening . . .': the lines are from 'Love Among the Ruins' (1855) by Robert Browning (1812-89)

Chapter 6. Crème de menthe

At the Pompadour Gerald finds Birkin drinking with a girl called Minette, a beautiful but sullen model who is between jobs and, apparently, between men. Birkin tells her about Gerald's career as soldier, explorer and (now) mine-manager. Gerald feels 'an awful, enjoyable power' over her, a lust mixed with cruelty; she seems to him 'a victim'. They are joined by a dark, slim young man with a high-pitched voice, called Halliday. His attitude to Minette, who has been his mistress, is peevish and, she says, mindless. She is pregnant and considers having a child 'beastly'. There is a raffish jaded immorality about Halliday and his friends. Minette claims that she is not afraid of blood; someone asks her if she has ever seen blood and she stabs him in the hand. Halliday is taken out to be sick by Maxim, a young Russian, the only one present who seems sober. The party moves on by taxi to Halliday's home, where an Arab servant is treated contemptuously. Gerald's attention is caught by a wood-carving from the Pacific, showing a woman in labour, suggesting 'the extreme of physical sensation, beyond the limits of mental consciousness'. He wonders if the piece is obscene. Soon afterwards everyone goes to bed.

NOTES AND GLOSSARY:
the Madonna: a work for which Minette—incongruously—has been the model
Crème de menthe: a mint liqueur, rich and sticky

Chapter 7. Totem

Gerald wakes beside Minette who is still asleep; her defencelessness excites him once more. He joins Halliday and Maxim Libidnikov who are sitting naked by the fire. Halliday praises nudism. Gerald thinks it undignified, but he enjoys feeling free for once from respectability. Birkin praises the art of the statuette which Gerald noticed last night: it belongs to a culture which is purely sensual, he explains.

Gerald stays for several days. Finally he quarrels with Halliday and is on the point of punching him. He leaves, regretting only that he has not paid Minette. Gerald reflects that he is a whole man, the others— Birkin included—half-men. Minette will marry Halliday because a half-man is what she wants.

NOTES AND GLOSSARY:
Pietà: a composition showing the Virgin with the crucified Christ
comme il faut: (*French*) respectable

Chapter 8. Breadalby

Early in the summer Ursula and Gudrun visit Hermione at Breadalby, a fine old house in the Derbyshire countryside. The other guests include Birkin and Gerald; Sir Joshua Mattheson, a sociologist; Sir Alexander Roddice, Hermione's brother and a Member of Parliament; an Italian countess; and a German girl. Ursula feels unhappy at the clever but shallow conversation in this upper-class, cultured, cosmopolitan company.

The bond between Hermione and Birkin is under strain. She ridicules and belittles him. During a discussion of education, they quarrel when Hermione talks about the freedom she finds in knowing things— especially in her knowledge of the stars. Knowledge is like bottling up freedom, Birkin asserts. When she proposes a walk after tea, he refuses to join in and she calls him 'a sulky boy'. She wants to dominate him; she asks what he sees as he copies a Chinese drawing of geese. When he tells her that he can enter the being and blood of the geese, she thinks him 'devilish'. At times she enjoys the conflict but gradually she becomes frantic with hatred. They disagree next day when the guests discuss social reform; Hermione believes that 'we are all equal in spirit'; Birkin insists that he is 'separate' in spirit. Being contradicted wounds Hermione.

Birkin regrets his roughness and goes, penitently, to her room. Hermione is overwhelmed by a wish to 'break him down' and strikes at his head with a heavy paperweight; he fends off her second blow with a book. Hermione sleeps after this, and wakes feeling justified. Birkin, stunned, goes out into the country where he rolls naked among flowers and branches, tired of people and uniting himself with nature. He leaves Hermione a note telling her she was right to 'biff' him. He is ill for two weeks, but he has—almost—freed himself from her cloying influence.

The house-party is dominated by these developments between the two strongest personalities present. Other relationships are advanced, less dramatically, in the course of the formal meals and amusements—which include an improvised ballet and a morning swim. Gerald is increasingly attracted by Gudrun, although he regards her as a social inferior, and Birkin is 'drawn' to Ursula. Ursula's dislike of Hermione grows. Gerald and Birkin have adjacent rooms; they discuss the Brangwen sisters and the people they met in London. Gerald comments that Minette is 'rather foul'. Marriage, says Birkin, is his way to salvation.

NOTES AND GLOSSARY:

Georgian: a harmonious style of architecture dating from the eighteenth-century reigns of King George I, II and III

Corinthian pillars: a classical style with ornate capitals

Meredith . . . : the novels of George Meredith (1828–1909) are suggested by the presence of a lordly politician in a country house

Disraeli: Benjamin Disraeli (1804–81), a romantic figure, was Prime Minister in the 1870s

Darien: the Pacific Ocean was first sighted from a peak in Darien, Central America, as related in a sonnet by John Keats (1795–1821)

Fathers and Sons: a novel (1862) by the Russian author Ivan Turgenev (1818–83)

Vergini delle Rocchette: a story (1896) by the Italian author Gabriele d'Annunzio (1863–1938); three daughters of a prince are courted in an enchanted garden

Pavlova and Nijinsky: Anna Pavlova (1882–1931) and Vaslav Nijinsky (1890–1950) were the greatest Russian dancers

Naomi, Ruth, Orpah: when Naomi returned home from Moab, her widowed daughter-in-law Ruth followed her, but Orpah remained. See the Bible, Ruth

Integer vitae scelerisque purus: (*Latin*) a man whose life is beyond reproach and untainted by crimes: a line from the poet Horace (65–8BC)

Render Unto Caesarina: Christ said, 'Render unto Caesar the things which are Caesar's'. See the Bible, Matthew 22:21

Dionysus: Greek god of wine and revelry

Herr Obermeister . . . : German titles referring to function

Alexander Selkirk: a sailor (1676–1721) who was shipwrecked for several years; his experiences inspired Daniel Defoe (1660–1731) to write his best-known work, *Robinson Crusoe* (1720)

Chapter 9. Coal-dust

Going home from school, the sisters watch Gerald forcing his terrified Arab mare to stand at the railway crossing while a goods-train roars by. Ursula is horrified. Gudrun is shocked but excited. She screams at Gerald, 'I should think you're proud'. Ursula complains to the railway-crossing keeper about Gerald's cruelty. Gudrun is numbed by her memory of the man's body controlling the mare.

Two workers watch the girls pass by in their brilliant clothes. One tells the other he would give a week's pay for five minutes with Gudrun. Sensing his lust, Gudrun feels loathing. But she is attracted by the mining community. Like any miner's lass she likes to walk out on Friday evenings with a young man. But Gudrun feels stifled.

NOTES AND GLOSSARY:

Daphne: in Greek mythology, she was turned into a laurel tree when fleeing from Apollo

bloods: young men of fashion

Chapter 10. Sketch-book

One morning the sisters are sketching by Willey Water when Hermione and Gerald come up in a boat. Hermione greets Gudrun and insists on seeing her sketch-book. Gerald recalls Gudrun's words by the railway. As he reaches for the book it falls in the water. When Gudrun repels Hermione's effusive apologies, Gerald is impressed by her spirit. A look passes between them and a bond is formed.

Chapter 11. An island

Ursula wanders down the bank of a stream and meets Birkin working on a punt by a mill-pond. He takes her over to a small island, where they talk. He is pleased by the thought of an uncontaminated world, empty of people; but Ursula knows that humanity has a long way still to go. She dislikes the prophetic side of Birkin and also his 'Sunday-school' self-righteousness, but his 'freedom' and vitality delight her. When he says that Hermione wants to help him furnish his new rooms at the mill-house, Ursula is jealous.

NOTES AND GLOSSARY:

Paul et Virginie: very pure young lovers in a romance (1787) by the French author Bernardin de St Pierre (1737–1814)

Watteau: Antoine Watteau (1684–1721) was a French painter of delightful pastoral scenes, including picnics and dancing

Salvator Mundi: Saviour of the World

Ark of the Covenant: a sacred Temple chest containing relics, in ancient Jerusalem

Chapter 12. Carpeting

In the mill-house Hermione, asserting herself, measures the floors and compels Birkin to accept an expensive Persian camel-hair rug, though he doesn't want to take it. Over a picnic they talk about will-power, which Hermione claims is the secret of her success: Gerald, she says, was right to impose his will on his horse. Ursula is still indignant about that. Birkin decides that women, like horses, have two wills—one to submit and the other to bolt. Ursula considers herself as a bolter. She defends the horse's rights again, and goes home 'in arms' against the others. She will fight Birkin, to the death or to a new life.

NOTES AND GLOSSARY:

Fabre: Jean Henri Fabre (1823–1915), a distinguished French naturalist

Chapter 13. Mino

Birkin sends Ursula a note inviting the sisters to tea; Ursula decides to go alone. When she arrives, Birkin tells her that they must pledge themselves for ever, as friends at least. He doesn't know whether he loves her. He wants a more profound relationship than love: a balance between two single beings, like that of stars. Ursula is offended; she believes in love.

They watch the antics of two cats, Birkin's tom chivying a stray female. Ursula is angered by Birkin's defence of male superiority; his cat is like Gerald with his mare, she says. The tom is right, Birkin decides, to want a stable relationship. They continue to discuss Birkin's theory of balance between the sexes. Ursula tells him about her first love-affair with an officer, Skrebensky [treated in *The Rainbow*]. He thinks her reckless and exciting. She asks him to say the words 'my love' and—simply, for once—he does.

NOTES AND GLOSSARY:

Wille zur Macht: (*German*) will to power. Nietzsche's belief in an ethic of the strong is dismissed here by Birkin. Lawrence used to say that nothing made him more angry than bullying

---

Chapter 14. Water-party

Mr Crich gives a lake-party every year; this time the Brangwen family are invited. On the way Ursula and Gudrun, excited, infuriate their father by laughing helplessly at their mother's stately manner in her black and purple outfit. The sisters are brilliantly dressed as usual, and unconcerned about what people think of them. Their parents feel shy and awkward.

The girls borrow a canoe and find a lonely place where they bathe naked, picnic, and feel perfectly happy. Ursula sings in German. When Birkin and Gerald join them, Gudrun is dancing before a herd of bullocks. Birkin dances for Ursula. Gudrun races at the bullocks, alarming Gerald: the cattle can be deadly, he tells her. She strikes him on the face—'the first blow', he says. 'And I shall strike the last', she replies. A few moments later he tells her he loves her.

Birkin reflects on love and death, modern reality, dissolution, and the end of the world. When darkness falls they kindle decorated lanterns: Ursula's depict a moon and a sea-bed with crabs; Gudrun's flowers and a cuttle-fish with a cold gaze which frightens her. Gerald and Gudrun kiss and set off in the canoe, watching the fireworks and lanterns on the lake. She is in love with him now, and for the first time in his life he relaxes the tense will by which he normally lives. The boat drifts.

Suddenly there is shouting. Gerald's sister Diana has fallen overboard; a young doctor has gone in after her. Gerald, recalled to practical duties, goes to the rescue—in vain. When hope is lost, Birkin urges him to go home. The sluice is opened to drain the lake. Birkin talks on about death, like Hamlet—as he says himself. When he kisses Ursula and she clings to him, he feels a strong desire for her which leaves him upset and disturbed. Gerald remains at the lake, against his friend's advice. The dead bodies are found next morning; Diana, clinging in panic to the young doctor, has caused his death.

NOTES AND GLOSSARY:

Regarde, regarde . . .: (*French*) Look at them! Aren't they incredible owls!

Dalcroze: Emile Jacques-Dalcroze (1865–1950), a Swiss who invented a system of movements to interpret music, known as 'eurhythmics'

Ignis fatuus: (*Latin*) foolish fire, a phosphorescent light seen over marshes

sea-born Aphrodite: the Greek goddess of love was born from the foam of the sea

fleurs du mal: (*French*) flowers of evil, the title of a volume of poems (1857) by Charles Baudelaire (1821–67)

Chapter 15. Sunday evening

Ursula, profoundly depressed, broods about death. Suicide is repulsive but death has a romantic attraction: it seems pure. School starts again tomorrow and her life appears pointlessly mechanical; death would be an adventure. Birkin's talk has morbidly affected her.

Birkin arrives as the Brangwen children, Billy and Dora, are going to bed. Ursula sees his gentleness with Billy, kissing him goodnight; but she tells him he looks offensively ill: he ought to look after himself. He leaves, after her parents' return from church, and Ursula suffers an irrational hatred of him which lasts for days.

NOTES AND GLOSSARY:

Sappho: Greek poetess of the seventh century BC who, according to legend, threw herself into the sea for love

de trop: (*French*) unwelcome, in the way

Chapter 16. Man to man

On his sick-bed Birkin contemplates the prospect of marriage and domesticity, without enthusiasm. He is dissatisfied with everything except the idea of freedom. Women are possessive. They want to be dominant, like the ancient goddess, Great Mother of all things. The thought of woman as a maternal tyrant horrifies him. A man and a woman should not be broken fragments of a whole; a man should have his 'pure' freedom, a woman hers.

Gerald visits him; he is still fond of Birkin and is now protective towards him, but can't take him seriously as a man. He talks about Gudrun and about his family's reaction to Diana's death. Winifred, his younger sister, needs a teacher—perhaps Gudrun? They talk about education. Gerald hated school but is reluctant to question English methods. Birkin proposes a blood-brotherhood of eternal friendship: Gerald is uncertain about this.

NOTES AND GLOSSARY:

Magna Mater: (*Latin*) the Great Mother, a pagan goddess

Mater Dolorosa: (*Latin*) Mother of Sorrows; a name given to the mother of Christ

Orinoco: a tributary of the River Amazon

Timor mortis conturbat me: (*Latin*) the fear of death troubles me, an old refrain

Blutbrüderschaft: (*German*) blood-brotherhood

Chapter 17. The industrial magnate

Ursula forgets Birkin for a time and resumes her old interests and friendships. Gudrun is planning to go abroad. They visit a Mrs Kirk who was once Gerald's nurse. He was a little demon as a child, she recalls.

At Shortlands Mr Crich is dying. He has always tried to serve both God and his own workers—infuriating his wife by his charity. She has submitted to him but remained apart in spirit, like a 'moping dishevelled hawk'. Mr Crich has given his love to Winifred, a sensitive, strange child, now about thirteen. He is hoping that Gudrun will agree to leave her school post and come to look after her.

His father's condition unsettles Gerald; they have never been at ease together. When young, Gerald was attracted by dreams of adventure, war and 'savagery'—alternatives to his father's benevolent, responsible management of the family business. Travel has calmed him. Back home from exploring the Amazon he took over the mines and reorganised them on scientific principles, making them more efficient but less humane than under Mr Crich's control. He has always needed hard work to occupy his life. Women have brought him occasional relief but he no longer wants casual relationships with women.

NOTES AND GLOSSARY:

Homer . . . Odyssey: the *Odyssey*, an epic of travel and adventure by the Greek poet Homer (who lived about 900BC), was standard reading for boys

sati: in the past, Indian widows often sacrificed themselves on their husbands' funeral pyres

Chapter 18. Rabbit

Gudrun goes to Shortlands to take charge of Winifred. They make sketches of Winifred's pets. The huge rabbit, Bismarck, resists, 'demon-like', struggling and scratching, until Gerald tames it with a blow to the neck that makes it scream and cower. Gerald and Gudrun are excited. There is an unpredictable, perhaps vicious element in their relationship.

NOTES AND GLOSSARY:

sang-froid: (*French*) coolness, composure

Winifred veut faire . . .: (*French*) the French governess asks what Bismarck is. Gudrun tells her: a big, white and black rabbit

Bismarck: Otto von Bismarck (1815–98) was the first Chancellor of the German Empire, established in 1871

Chapter 19. Moony

Birkin (who has a private income) goes to the South of France to recover from his illness. Ursula feels unhappy and lost. On the evening of his return she finds him throwing stones at the moon's reflection in the mill-pond, and cursing the ancient goddess, Mother of all Things, whom he associates with it. Ursula begs him to stop. She tells him his attitude is one-sided: he wants her to serve him. Birkin says that the female ego is a rag doll; he wants her to give up her assertive will. Mockingly he says that 'do you love me?' is her battle-cry. But soon, although Birkin is determined not to make love, they are nestling together, kissing.

Next day Birkin thinks he may have been wrong. Perhaps he talks too much. He continues to meditate. An African statuette at Halliday's, delightfully elegant, comes to mind: it represents thousands of years of a purely sensual culture, he thinks. Northern peoples must develop in a different way. He recognises the mysterious character of such movements of civilisation, and thinks instead of Gerald, seeing him as a 'strange white demon' from the north, perhaps fated to a death by coldness.

Suddenly there is a way out of this labyrinth of thoughts and fancies. He believes in a personal integrity beyond all emotions—including love and desire—which combines independence with obligations to others. He must ask Ursula to marry him.

Ursula is out when he arrives. He tells her father that he means to propose. They wait uneasily, Will Brangwen irritated by Birkin. When Ursula comes home, she protests that she won't be bullied into anything. Will Brangwen thinks her contrary and is furious.

Ursula discusses marriage with Gudrun; they are still close but conscious now of differences. Ursula is protective towards men, Gudrun is respectful but fearful of them. Ursula decides that she will accept Birkin only if he is prepared to love her absolutely. Although he hates the thought of self-abandonment, she is prepared to fight him for it.

NOTES AND GLOSSARY:

Cybele . . . Dea Syria: the ancient Mother-goddess who represents, to Birkin, woman's instinct to dominate
Girl's Own: a children's periodical
Lloyd George: David Lloyd George (1863–1945), a British politician

Chapter 20. Gladiatorial

Birkin is angry with Ursula. He goes to Gerald at Shortlands and finds him, uncharacteristically, bored; they discuss cures for boredom; Birkin suggests work, love and fighting. They agree to do some Japanese wrestling and, stripped naked, tangle on the carpet. Birkin throws Gerald. Afterwards they are exhilarated; Birkin decides that physical contact is good for preserving sanity. He tells Gerald about Ursula's refusal. Gerald doubts if he will ever truly love.

NOTES AND GLOSSARY:

Bokhara: a region in Russian Turkestan
on the *qui vive:* (*French*) on the alert

Chapter 21. Threshold

After a London exhibition of her wood-carvings Gudrun is welcomed back to Shortlands. Winifred gives her flowers. Mr Crich has promised to provide an artists' studio at the house. He likes Gudrun to sit with him; she keeps him in touch with life. Gerald is appalled by his father's struggle with death. Winifred disregards it, and the old man tries to do the same. Although living close to a deathbed, Gudrun feels a sudden, frenzied desire for Gerald. She imagines ancient Roman orgies and speaks critically of the vagueness of Birkin's theories about marriage.

NOTES AND GLOSSARY:

mauvaise honte: (*French*) bashfulness
Laocoön: a Trojan priest who was crushed with his two sons by a sea-serpent
while Rome burns: Nero, the Roman emperor (AD54–68), is said to have fiddled while the city was in flames

Chapter 22. Woman to woman

Ursula goes to tea with Birkin. He is out but Hermione is there. Ursula complains about Birkin's idea of a marriage beyond love; she scarcely understands it. Jealous of Ursula, Hermione tells her that Birkin is not strong enough to make her a good husband. Birkin arrives and tries to placate them. Hermione shows off her knowledge of Italy and speaks Italian to the cat. Ursula feels excluded and leaves in anger.

NOTES AND GLOSSARY:

an odalisk: a Turkish slave-girl
si jeunesse savait: (*French*) if youth only knew!
fat: (*French*) fop
in rhapsodic manner . . .: Hermione begins to speak about the enthusiasm of young Italians for new causes; a moment later she asks the cat if it remembers her—it certainly understands Italian, its mother's language; it is a fine boy, taught bad manners; it mustn't put its paw in the saucer . . .

Chapter 23. Excurse

Next day is a half-day for Ursula; Birkin calls at her school and asks her out for a drive in the afternoon. In the car he gives her three rings (which don't fit). Ursula is happy until he announces that he must say goodbye to Hermione at Shortlands at tea-time; then, in a fit of jealousy, she calls Hermione 'a fish-wife', tells Birkin that his talk of truth and purity stinks, throws the rings at him and walks off up the road. When she comes back she gives him a flower.

They drive to Southwell and have tea near the Minster, forgetting Hermione. She thinks him like one of the sons of God in the Bible who loved the daughters of men. Birkin wants to wander the world with her. They write letters of resignation from their jobs, and, truly united, spend a night together in Sherwood Forest. They wake laughing and thrilled by something more than love: a sense of the night and of mystery.

NOTES AND GLOSSARY:
Sons of God: see Genesis 6:1–4; heroes are born from these unions
Southwell . . . Sherwood Forest: places in Nottinghamshire

Chapter 24. Death and love

Gerald is frightened by his father's approaching death. His mother urges him to look after himself. Walking Gudrun home, he tells her that he cares for nothing but her. He kisses her, under a bridge where the miners take their sweethearts; she enjoys reflecting that he is the miners' master.

Mr Crich dies. Winifred is taken away to London. After days of loneliness Gerald visits his father's grave and then steals into Gudrun's room, with clay from the grave still on his boots. Leaving in the dawn he is comforted and happy, but Gudrun feels old and is glad to be rid of him. Their night together has not been such a union as that of Ursula and Birkin in the forest.

NOTES AND GLOSSARY:
Damocles: a sword was suspended by a hair, above his head, at an ancient Sicilian court banquet, to show him the happiness known to kings
en ménage: (*French*) domesticated
nowt: nothing. The spelling in this passage reproduces the miner's accent and dialect

---

Chapter 25. Marriage or not

The Brangwens are to move house. Ursula puts off deciding on a day for the wedding.

Gerald speaks to Birkin about his own hopes of marrying Gudrun. Birkin is unenthusiastic. He dislikes 'the world all in couples'. He believes in something broader: a perfect friendship between two men in addition to marriage. Gerald declines this offer.

The chapter ends with an explanation of Gerald's position. He is approaching marriage without sincerely committing himself to Gudrun.

If he were able to commit himself to Birkin he might later achieve a 'mystic marriage' with Gudrun.

NOTES AND GLOSSARY:

pis-aller: (*French*) last resource
égoïsme à deux: (*French*) two equally selfish people

Chapter 26. A chair

Ursula and Birkin buy an antique chair in a sale at the market. Birkin praises the early nineteenth century when such craftsmanship was still possible, but Ursula is annoyed by his love of the past and they give the chair away to a young workman and his fiancée. The girl is pregnant; the couple are obliged to make a home—no chance for them of foreign travel. The young man looks 'rat-like' to Ursula, a product of modern urban life at its worst. But Birkin insists that the world in future will belong to such ordinary folk; exceptional people like the Birkins will have to live among them as well as they can. Ursula now agrees to be married, though she remains worried by his wish for more than just a wife. He still wants an ideal friendship too.

NOTES AND GLOSSARY:

Poiret: Paul Poiret (1879–1944), French designer and decorator
Rodin: Auguste Rodin (1840–1917), French sculptor
Michael Angelo: Michelangelo Buonarroti (1475–1564), Italian painter, sculptor, architect and poet
the meek: see the Bible, Matthew 5:5

Chapter 27. Flitting

When Ursula announces at home that she means to be married next day, her parents resent being excluded from her plans. Her father smacks her face and she goes to Birkin in tears. She has loved her father but it has been a love of opposition, he tells her. They marry next day and Birkin makes her write to her parents. Her mother replies; her father does not. Meanwhile, Birkin feels reborn. Ursula advises Gerald to propose to Gudrun. He hopes at least to go abroad with her at Christmas. Birkin thinks Gudrun is a 'born mistress'.

The Brangwen family have moved. The sisters go to the old house to fetch Ursula's things. Contemplating the bare rooms, Gudrun senses that a normal, settled marriage would be intolerable. Next day Gudrun goes to her sister upset because Gerald has been discussing their plans for a holiday with Birkin. Ursula reassures her: it shows that Gudrun means more to him than any of his girls in London.

NOTES AND GLOSSARY:
bêtise des voisins: (*French*) stupidity of the neighbours
type: (*French*) type; common person

Chapter 28. Gudrun in the Pompadour

Christmas approaches. Gerald and Gudrun are to meet the Birkins in Austria. On the way they spend an evening at the Pompadour. Minette is there and makes it clear that she has been Gerald's mistress. Halliday and his friends drunkenly read aloud from one of Birkin's letters, ridiculing the religiosity of his style and ideas. Gudrun puts a stop to this, borrowing the letter and then marching out with it. Gerald is surprised by how strongly she reacts.

NOTES AND GLOSSARY:
Lord, what must I do to be saved?: see the Bible, Mark 10:17 and Acts 16:30

Chapter 29. Continental

The Birkins, exulting in their departure from England, make the long boat and train journey to Austria, arriving at their Innsbruck hotel by sledge over the snow. 'Mr and Mrs Crich' are already there. At dinner they talk about how conventional the English are. Birkin is glad to be abroad. They go on next day to a hostel in the mountains. Gudrun is sensitive to the isolation; she feels 'lost' when Gerald makes love to her.

They meet the other guests. In a boisterous dance, Gudrun partners a fair youth called Leitner who is the companion of a weird-looking sculptor, Herr Loerke. Gerald dances with a Professor's daughter; his pleasure in his power to attract the girl is obvious to Gudrun; she noticed this love of conquest when they broke their journey in Paris. She decides that Gerald is naturally promiscuous and that she must fight him. In the bedroom she is frightened, though she hides it with a ruse.

Gerald excels at winter sports. Indoors, Gudrun gets to know Loerke —whom Gerald and Birkin detest—pleased by his stories of early poverty and by his aesthetic ideas. Art, he believes, is separate from life; she agrees. He shows her a picture of a statuette he once made in green bronze, representing Lady Godiva as a young girl, naked on a great horse. She takes Loerke's side when this work is discussed.

Ursula wants to leave; the snow pains her. Gudrun presents her with coloured stockings; but they are growing apart. Ursula has accepted Birkin's ideals; her sister cannot go beyond love because she has never reached it—so Ursula says. Gerald confesses that he can hardly bear his passion for Gudrun, and Birkin offers his friendship in support. Desperate and bewildered by Gudrun's behaviour, Gerald replies sceptically. The Birkins go south to Italy.

NOTES AND GLOSSARY:

deuxième classe . . .: (*French*) they have half an hour before taking their second class seats

La vie, c'est une affaire . . .: (*French*) life is for those with imperial souls

tant pis pour moi: (*French*) the worse for me!

Kuchen: (*German*) cake

prachtvoll . . .: (*German*) all these words mean 'wonderful'

Reunionsaal: (*German*) common-room

Herr Professor . . .: (*German*) Professor, may I present . . . Will you join us?

Das war ausgezeichnet . . .: (*German*) Excellent!

das ist wirklich schade . . .: (*German*) that is really a shame!

wie schön, wie rührend . . .: (*German*) Beautiful! Moving! Such spirit in these Scottish songs. The lady has such a voice, an artist!

Prosit: (*German*) a toast: good health

Mene! Mene!: a warning which appeared, written on a wall, to Belshazzar, King of Babylon; see the Bible, Daniel 5:24–8

ein schönes Frauenzimmer: (*German*) a lovely girl, a 'smasher'

Parnell: Charles Stewart Parnell (1846–91), political advocate of Irish independence, whose career was wrecked by his liaison with Katherine O'Shea

Mach mich auf . . .: (*German*) Make me a fire, I'm wet from the rain

Lady Godiva: legendary Anglo-Saxon lady who rode naked through Coventry to save the city from a levy

Maud Allan: (1883–1956) a dancer, often scantily clad

'Nor pine for what is not': '*And* pine' is what Shelley wrote in 'Ode to a Skylark' (1819)

Chapter 30. Snowed up

The conflict between Gerald and Gudrun now frightens them both. His love seems to her like a frost. She forces him to say that he can't love her, then that he does. She humiliates him, admitting to Loerke, in his presence, that they are not married. The curious, perverse flirtation which she develops with the sculptor leads to the catastrophe. She and Gerald make arrangements to part, and she goes tobogganing with Loerke. Gerald meets them, knocks Loerke down, almost strangles Gudrun, and goes off alone into the snow to his death.

NOTES AND GLOSSARY:

Mestrovic: Ivan Mestrovic (1883–1962) Yugoslavian sculptor

Bitte sagen Sie . . . : (*German*) Please don't keep saying 'Dear Lady'; *'Frau'* is the form for a married woman. Gerald strikes Loerke when he calls Gudrun *'Gnädiges Fräulein'*, the form of address for an unmarried girl

Goethe . . . : Johann Wolfgang von Goethe (1749–1832), the German poet and scientist, lived at Weimar; he met J.C.F. von Schiller (1759–1805), dramatist and poet, in 1794. Jean-Jacques Rousseau (1712–78) and Voltaire (François Marie Arouet, 1694–1778) were French intellectuals of the time of Frederick II of Prussia (1712–86) who befriended Voltaire

Don Juan: proverbial Spanish seducer

Hetty Sorrel . . . : she is seduced by Arthur Donnithorne in George Eliot's novel *Adam Bede* (1859)

The Great Rachel: Elisa Félix Rachel (1820–58), French actress of such parts

---

Chapter 31. Exeunt

Ursula and her husband return, to find an emotionless Gudrun. Birkin is deeply moved. If Gerald had loved him, it would have made a difference, he believes. Gudrun goes to Dresden. The body is taken home. The Birkins return to the mill. Ursula asks, isn't she enough for him? Did he need Gerald? He insists that he did.

NOTES AND GLOSSARY:

Il est mort?: (*French*) He is dead?

Imperial Caesar . . . : *Hamlet*, Act 5, scene i

the Kaiser: Wilhelm II of Germany (1859–1941; ruled 1888–1918); his words mean 'I didn't want it'

Part 3

Commentary

Nature, purpose and achievement

In the autumn of 1916 Lawrence wrote excitedly to friends about the newly-completed *Women in Love*: 'it is a terrible . . . and wonderful novel'; 'I know it is true . . . The world of my novel is big and fearless— yes, I love it . . .'; 'the book frightens me: it is so end of the world. But it is, it must be, the beginning of a new world too'; 'it is the book of my free soul'. These and other passages from letters* express his sense of having stretched his own talents and challenged the world. *Women in Love* conveys the fear, excitement and wonder to be felt in these letters; it offers a remarkable man's personal view of life; it extends the scope and technique of English fiction; and it achieves what novelists have always aimed at—a vivid impression of human relationships against the social background of their time.

Lawrence believed that ugliness was the tragedy of England: industrial progress had brought ugliness into towns, houses, schools, and furniture; into marriage, work and all human affairs. Materialism was like a disease. 'Nag, nag, nag' about politics and money, he complained, was all the modern English were fit for. On one occasion he called *Women in Love* 'purely destructive', and although it is not that, it is an attack on materialism and on the utilitarian outlook of twentieth-century industrialism. Ugliness was made worse by the war; 1916 was an alarming year, and not only for those directly involved in the fighting. The nineteenth century's confidence in progress and order was dwindling fast among intellectuals. The doubts and panic of an un-settled decade were starkly expressed in *Women in Love*, making it (as Lawrence said) 'terrible', and frightening even to its author.

Nonetheless, Lawrence was enthusiastic about novel-writing, and about what might be done to start a new world. According to myth the phoenix, his emblem, died in fire and was born again. In spite of its pessimism, *Women in Love* reflects the exuberance of a confident artist. It offers a vision of personal freedom in marriage and friendship.

*see *D.H. Lawrence: A Critical Anthology*, edited by H. Coombes, 'Penguin Critical Anthologies', Penguin Books, Harmondsworth, 1973, pp.104–15. Other letters referred to below can be found in full here.

Although Birkin's beliefs may at first seem irrelevant (as Gerald thinks them) to the social problem which Lawrence saw as 'ugliness', novels have always made marriage and personal relations central to their picture of everything else. Birkin's view of marriage is a plea for emancipation, for men and women; it leads to his dislike of possessions (Hermione has tried to possess him). A responsible freedom (not the licence of Halliday and his circle) is the only way, Birkin and Lawrence assert, to resist the dreary 'nagging' of the modern world. *Women in Love* is idealistic and challenging, as Lawrence intended.

The novel is often difficult on first encounter. The main characters were found offensive when the book was published. Violence, emotional tension, despair, and over-excitement make their behaviour appear abnormal to readers used to nineteenth-century fiction. Lawrence replied that his people were *'alive'*. He wanted to portray relations between men and women without the reticence which earlier writers had accepted as a law of fiction. The sexual frankness of many novelists today makes *Women in Love* seem almost restrained, but in 1916 old-fashioned readers would have thought even the title shocking. The Professor's daughter who dances with Gerald at the Austrian hostel is said to be 'almost dying of virgin excitement'; she is 'palpitating', 'fluttering, flushing'; she shrinks 'convulsively . . . violently' (Chapter 29, p.463) and can scarcely speak afterwards. Gudrun is thrilled by the sight of Gerald's 'loins'. Ursula clings to Birkin's 'loins'. Even when describing hazel catkins or a mining landscape, the novel's language is erotically charged; the sisters, walking past the miners' houses, undergo the 'violation of a dark, uncreated, hostile world' (Chapter 1, p.13). The lustful workman in Chapter 9 speaks very bluntly about what he would like to do with Gudrun. Lawrence was deliberately flouting the censors. He risked prosecution, and he helped to free English literature from what had become a tiresome prudishness.

Sexual impulse is only a part of his recognition of the complex experience of men and women in love. Birkin is bashful in courting Ursula (in Chapter 14); Gerald relishes power over Minette (in Chapter 6); a shared pleasure in violence unites Gerald and Gudrun; and Ursula vacillates between hatred and love of Birkin before their marriage. The aggressive and fearful undercurrents of human nature, discussed during these years by Freud, are explicit in *Women in Love*.

Lawrence was not a Freudian, though he thought Freud interesting, and was perhaps influenced by Freud in rejecting 'the old stable *ego* of the character' (in traditional fiction). He saw that people are less consistent and predictable than Victorian characterisation allows for. He refused to see character purely in social terms: John Galsworthy (1867–

1937), Lawrence considered, wrote about social rather than human beings. The rabbit Bismarck is 'a mystery' (Chapter 18) and a human being is even more so. Lawrence wanted to reveal the presence of mysterious 'forces of life'—including 'dark', 'underworld' forces—in the make-up of his characters. When he called his book 'big and fearless', he had this in mind. (See the section on Characters, p.44.)

A new conception of integrity in character required experiment with technique. Lawrence rejected plot and 'contrivance' in favour of organic structure; a novel was to be shaped by its own inner nature. When *Women in Love* first appeared some critics thought it formless. 'A book which is not a copy of other books has its own construction' he wrote; what an imitator might consider 'faults' he would call 'characteristics'. Obviously any novel has to be planned and may have faults, but Lawrence was right to emphasise that he was no imitator. The 'characteristics' of *Women in Love* are considered in the sections on Structure and Style which follow.

J.I.M. Stewart has pointed out in *Eight Modern Writers** the extent to which the novel is conventional: it uses a country-house party to assemble its characters; a story of two sisters and their young men is likely to remind us of Jane Austen's *Pride and Prejudice* (1813) and George Eliot's *Middlemarch* (1871-2); taking the main characters abroad for the final chapters is an old device. *Women in Love* is effective in many ways that are equally traditional: in its landscapes of the Midland countryside spoiled by the mines; in its minor characters, like Gerald's old nurse, or Winifred with her pets; and in its picturing of English society in transition.

Background to composition

The background is the life of an invalid writer in wartime. *Women in Love* is a war novel in the sense that it reflects Lawrence's reactions to war conditions: 'the results of one's soul of the war', he said. At times of despair he felt that the 'iron rain' of war would destroy the world like a second Flood. The ruling class, represented by Gerald in the novel, appeared to be destroying itself. At home war conditions intensified everything that Lawrence hated about England. He wanted to leave, to found a community in America where (with a few friends) 'decent' living might be possible.

Few writers can have had more contempt for the public than Lawrence in 1916. *The Rainbow* had been suppressed. He had been abused

*Oxford University Press, 1963; Oxford University Press Paperback, 1973, p.513. Page references below are to the 1973 edition.

in the press. He could not publish *Women in Love*. After the formation of a coalition government in 1915 and the conscription that followed, the authorities possessed extensive powers; in 1917 he was forced to leave Cornwall by military order. He sympathised with the working men who were conscripted while he was too ill to serve, but the masses frightened and horrified him. London seemed an inferno (as it does in the train, in Chapter 5 of the novel, to Birkin). England was no place then for an artist who dreamed of a new world; Lawrence took refuge from the war in literature.

He had no doubt about his own position there. When starting 'The Sisters' in 1913 he believed he could write 'bigger stuff than any man in England'. This was in a letter to Edward Garnett (1868–1937); Garnett and others in the literary world admired his work; Ezra Pound (1885–1972) thought him 'the best of the younger men'; another American, the poet Robert Frost (1874–1963), thought highly of his verse. Henry James was less enthusiastic, judging that Lawrence 'hung behind' H.G. Wells (1866–1946) and Arnold Bennett (1867–1931), 'in the dusty rear' (*Times Literary Supplement* 19 March 1914). Wells, Bennett, and Galsworthy were all, for Lawrence, 'imitators'; at least, they were less likely to offend the public than the author of *The Rainbow*, which John Galsworthy thought 'detestable'.

Lawrence found solace in a circle of literary friends. These included Aldous Huxley (1894–1963), the novelist and essayist whom he met in 1915; Bertrand Russell; and Lady Ottoline Morrell (1873–1938), the eccentric hostess of Garsington Manor, near Oxford, a house where she received Lawrence and where he met other writers and artists. Breadalby, in the novel, gives the reader some idea of what Garsington was like; Lady Ottoline believed Hermione Roddice to be a cruel picture of herself. Several other friends considered that Lawrence had put them into his book.

A *roman à clef* is a novel in which the characters are thinly disguised portraits from real life; *Women in Love* is more complex and imaginative than that. Lawrence always drew on his own experiences: the Pompadour café comes from his memories of the Café Royal in London; Chapter 28, 'Gudrun in the Pompadour', is based on an incident involving a Lawrence letter. Many other details have counterparts in the author's life; he knew of a colliery-owner's son who had accidentally shot his brother; he had seen an African statuette at the flat of a friend, Philip Heseltine (1894–1930), a musician who saw himself in the artist Halliday and tried to stop the novel's publication. Gerald and Gudrun owe something to the critic John Middleton Murry and Katherine Mansfield, the short-story writer; they were friends of Lawrence, who proposed 'blood-brotherhood' to Murry. Nonetheless, Murry failed to recognise himself; Lawrence insisted that Hermione was no more like Lady Ottoline than Queen Victoria. A creative writer transforms whatever he uses. Rupert Birkin is a self-portrait; but all the characters derive from the same imagination.

The immediate background to the novel's composition is the England Lawrence knew between 1913 and 1916. The characters are intellectuals, 'advanced' men and women, artists and teachers; behind them are the miners of the Midlands; he wrote about what he knew. The war accelerated change among all these people; it hastened—in the absence of men in the army—the availability of jobs and independence for women; it lowered social 'barriers'. But it was the horror of the war, in the author's mind, that gave the book its tone.

The structure

The staunchest supporter of Lawrence's reputation in the years after his death was the Cambridge critic F.R. Leavis (1895-1978). Leavis defended Lawrence's work in his journal *Scrutiny*, and wrote *D.H. Lawrence: Novelist* in 1955. He saw *Women in Love* as a dramatic poem, and compared its method to Shakespeare's. Leavis was inclined to overstate Lawrence's achievement, but there is something to be said for this comparison as a means of approach to the structure of *Women in Love*. Shakespeare fuses together story, themes and imagery; Lawrence aimed to do the same.

Contrast and connection are principles of structure; Lawrence wrote: 'the novel is the highest example of subtle inter-relatedness that man has discovered'.* In the later nineteenth century novelists using symbolism had tried to make every detail relate to the rest; connection and contrast mattered more to them than chronicling events. In the structure of *Women in Love* we can see such 'inter-relatedness' in relationships, themes and imagery.

The structure of relationships

One contrast dominates the novel: Birkin and Ursula succeed; Gerald and Gudrun fail. Their stories draw the reader on, but each relationship helps to explain the other, and this creates a sense of order. Birkin and Ursula are associated with life and renewal, Gerald and Gudrun with perversity and death.

*'Morality and the Novel', *Phoenix: the Posthumous Papers of D.H. Lawrence*, edited by E.D. McDonald, 1936; Penguin edition, 1978, p.528.

The two men are clearly contrasted. Birkin, though frail and sickly, is full of vitality. Ursula feels that 'the moulding of him was so quick and attractive, it gave such a great sense of freedom: the moulding of his brows, his chin, his whole physique, something so alive, somewhere, in spite of the look of sickness' (Chapter 11, p.144). Birkin is independent, and he loves spontaneity. We are meant to see his brooding about the doom of mankind as the reaction of a healthy mind to the deadliness of modern life. Gerald is the 'most wanting' of the Criches, so his mother believes (Chapter 2, p.28). It is frequently implied that his energy is wasted. 'Where does his *go* go to . . .?' asks Gudrun, in Chapter 4. 'It goes in applying the latest appliances', says Ursula (p.53). He has killed his brother in an accident; his devotion to mechanical work, Lawrence insists, is even more of a curse. He lives by will-power and is, insecurely, dependent on his mines, on girls like Minette, on his father, and on Birkin. We are not surprised when Birkin throws him in the wrestling match. The sisters have more in common, but Ursula has more respect for other lives than Gudrun has; Lawrence wants her to represent the right way for a woman to live. Gudrun is 'cold', like Gerald, and less well-balanced than her sister.

Birkin and Ursula struggle towards a relationship which satisfies Birkin's (and Lawrence's) theory of marriage; neither is to exploit the other; they are to be 'balanced', and so free. What this means is clearer as we watch Gerald and Gudrun. There is a possessiveness about Gerald's desire for Minette (he wants to pay her). He enjoys mastering animals—his horse and Winifred's rabbit. Gudrun is excited by that and likes to think that he is the miners' master, but she finally tires of submitting to him. Neither she nor Gerald is capable of Birkin's ideal of generous freedom and 'balance' in love. Birkin and Ursula have to work their way to, and (they hope) beyond, love; the others are unable to try.

Other relationships help to establish the structure of the novel: Hermione's attempt to dominate Birkin clarifies his concept of marriage, and her 'will for power' shows us what is wrong with Gerald and Gudrun. Gudrun's liking for Loerke, who sets art before life and is—to Birkin—'a little obscene monster' (Chapter 29, p.481), confirms the impression that her love for Gerald has been perverse and unreal. Birkin's friendship with Gerald is central: by refusing to take it as seriously as Birkin asks, Gerald reveals, we are told (Chapter 25, p.398) his inability to mature into a 'balanced' love for Gudrun. By insisting on his need for a 'blood-brotherhood', Birkin affirms his refusal to be possessed by the (motherly) Ursula. There is an obvious parallel between the sisters and the 'brothers': Ursula tells Gudrun in Chapter 27 that the men are 'like brothers' (p.427). We might see a connection between Ursula's jealousy of Hermione and Gerald's jealousy of Loerke; or another between two 'triangles': Hermione, Birkin, Ursula; Minette, Gerald, Gudrun. Relationships are so organised that we look for patterns, perhaps comparing the scene where Gudrun comforts Mr Crich in Chapter 21 with the awkward meeting of Birkin and Will Brangwen in Chapter 19; both fathers are out of touch with their eldest children.

Such patterns remind us of drama. Lawrence builds up his novel in a succession of major and minor scenes, many of which could easily be adapted for the stage. The two stories alternate as in a play, scenes with Ursula followed by scenes with Gudrun. We see the two sisters alone, talking about marriage (and men) as in Chapters 1, 4 and 19; large crowded scenes like the Breadalby visit or the party on the water bring all the major characters and relationships together. Love and friendship develop through moments of drama: Gudrun screams at Gerald that he is proud; she strikes him; Ursula throws the rings at Birkin, and returns with a flower; Gudrun taunts Gerald by dancing before the cattle; Hermione attacks Birkin with the paperweight; Birkin and Gerald wrestle together. There is nothing geometrical (this was a term of disapproval for Lawrence) in the patterns of relationships. *Women in Love* is full of drama, spectacle and surprise; it has been adapted successfully as a film.

Thematic structure

Lawrence distinguished firmly between 'life' and simple 'existence'. He hated the mechanised efficiency of modern industrial society because it restricted people to dreary apathy. In reorganising the mines, Gerald has established a 'perfect inhuman machine' (Chapter 18, p.257) and reduced the miners to 'mere mechanical instruments' (p.259). Expert men, following scientific methods, have taken control; the miners have become joyless, hopeless and incapable even of hatred, although they had rebelled against the benign regime of Mr Crich. Gerald is affected too by the mechanical system he has made of the old, warm 'warren' of the mines. Alone, after work, he feels afraid and unreal. Lawrence makes him represent technological progress, which Birkin challenges when he questions Gerald in the train to London, asking what material productivity will lead to: 'all the coal . . . and all the plush furniture, and pianofortes . . . and our bellies are filled . . . what then?' (Chapter 5, p.61). The theme of real life, as opposed to a materialism which makes 'mechanical instruments' of people, pervades the novel.

The contrasted relationships illustrate that Gerald and Gudrun resemble the ideal couple of commercial advertising: he is handsome and successiul at work; she is a lovely, talented girl, good with children and old people. Gudrun daydreams, in Austria, of what her life with Gerald could be like: he might become a Member of Parliament and 'clear up the great muddle of labour and industry . . . every problem could be worked out, in life as in geometry. And he would care neither about himself nor about anything but the pure working out of the problem. He was very pure, really' (Chapter 29, p.469). This purity does not satisfy her, though; it is cold and deathly. Birkin's effort to find a belief and live it out with Ursula involves a rejection of modern English conditions. Once united, they give up their jobs and renounce domesticity. Real life, Lawrence believed, must be sought outside England.

The settings develop the same theme. London is like hell to Birkin; Halliday's friends in the Pompadour have escaped from life. The café is a place of cynical 'existence', filled with smoke, reflected in the mirrors; it is 'a vague dim world of shadowy drinkers' (Chapter 6, p.68). The Midland countryside, defaced by the mines, is like 'a ghoulish replica of the real world' (Chapter 1, p.12). Shortlands has charm, but smoke from the mines can be seen from the house: it too is the product of Gerald's 'machine'. The country house Breadalby belongs to an earlier epoch, but looks, in twentieth-century England, like an old painting. The variety of settings helps to show the 'whole pulse of social England' (which Gudrun is said to have touched) and to reinforce the theme of England's decline.

Education is a theme continued from *The Rainbow*. Hermione in Ursula's classroom (in Chapter 3) questions whether the children are better for 'all this pulling to pieces, all this knowledge' (p.43). Birkin, like Lawrence, has had doubts about this, but he disagrees with her because he thinks that her abstract intellectualism is incompatible with proper living. Birkin is a teacher in all his relationships, and education in the novel is not confined to schoolroom scenes or discussions among the characters. Children and adults must be educated, Birkin believes; he wants to teach Gerald and Ursula how to live. Knowledge and mental skills can be dangerous. Gerald reads the latest books on science and philosophy; 'his mind was very active. But it was like a bubble floating in the darkness' (Chapter 18, p.261). Winifred, we are meant to feel, learns more in responding to the 'wonder' of her rabbit. False education is like Loerke's separation of art and life. The novel conveys Lawrence's almost religious view of 'life': art and education, when misconceived, endanger it. England is becoming a place of wrongly educated 'experts' in machinery, like those who take hope and joy out of the mines.

Love and death are a traditional pair in poetry and art. Lawrence counterpoints these themes. Mr Crich is dying as Gerald and Gudrun begin to fall in love. The death of Diana breaks in on the couples at the lake-party. The words (used in the title to Chapter 24) run throughout the book. Death is connected with the purity of the snow and cold which kill Gerald; real love is impure, involving all emotions and the whole body. Death haunts the lovers. Gerald is like Cain who killed his brother; Ursula yearns for death after the lake-party; Birkin broods about the death of England.

The themes which shape the book are interconnected and developed through the relationships. The language, imagery, and symbolism of *Women in Love* help to unify the novel on the level of poetry.

Poetic structure

Lawrence held that personality cannot be defined effectively in precise formulas, but is subject to mysterious forces of nature, best evoked in symbols, images, and keywords. Lawrence is inventive with images; Hermione is compared in a lively image to a fallen angel; behind that are the symbols of darkness and the underworld. Symbols could not be invented, he said; they lie in the human mind for centuries. *Women in Love* is traditional in its use of light and darkness, sky and sea, flowers, animals, lights, the moon, mountains and snow. Their bearing on character and theme is new.

Darknesss pervades the novel, and has many connotations. The mines are a dark underworld, and the mining town is 'a dark, uncreated, hostile world' (Chapter 1, p.13); the miners' houses are 'darkened'; there is a persisting 'glamour of blackness' in the countryside. London is a dark city: Birkin enters 'the tremendous shadow of the town' (Chapter 5, p.67); the Pompadour is dark with smoke. When Gudrun tells Gerald she cannot love him, in Chapter 30, her eyes are 'dark-filled' like 'two moons of darkness' (p.520). Loerke, says Birkin, is a 'monster of the darkness'; women, attracted to such men, 'creep down some ghastly tunnel of darkness' (Chapter 29, p.481). These are images of corruption, but darkness also signifies mystery, lying below and beyond the conscious mind, as when Ursula ponders death 'darkly' (Chapter 15, p.214). Desire and love are connected with the dark. Caressing Birkin's loins, Ursula touches 'the quick of the mystery of darkness that was bodily him' (Chapter 23, p.354); and their night in the forest which follows is 'an inheritance of dark reality' (p.361).

Lights and picture-lanterns break the darkness over the lake in Chapter 14. The moon's reflection which Birkin stones in Chapter 19 is an 'explosion' of light with a white-burning centre. The brightness of the Austrian snow is unbearable to Ursula; it seems to beat upon her and 'strangle her soul' (Chapter 29, p.488). Light and cold belong to Gerald who dies in the snow: Birkin thinks him 'one of those strange white wonderful demons from the north' (Chapter 19, p.286). The Arctic north, in his reverie in this chapter, is opposed to Africa: Halliday's African statuette suggests a sensual culture; Europe is abstract like the northern ice and snow. These images of the uncanny build up an impression of nature working in the characters' lives. The moon represents to Birkin the unchanging female powers recognised long ago in religions of a supreme goddess. 'Devil' and 'demon' are images—not always pejorative—which denote other forces of life: rebellion in the rabbit, 'the long demon-like beast' (Chapter 19, p.271); cold self-destructiveness in Gerald. Natural energy and potency is present in the horses which Gerald subdues and Loerke sculpts. The horse is a favourite Lawrence symbol. He gives impressions of people with animal images: the young man who is given the chair is like a rat in his 'stillness and silkiness' (Chapter 26, p.403). Flowers are emblems of love in Ursula's classroom, when Winifred gives a bouquet to Gudrun, who comes out of the rain 'like a flower just opened' (Chapter 21, p.315), and when Ursula accepts Birkin on the road with a flower of purple-red bell-heather.

Symbolist writing of this kind is evocative, and often enigmatic. The writing communicates the brute strength and delicate nature of the mare, and the colliery-train's metallic, mechanical clatter and rumble, grinding and squeaking: two separate worlds of nature and machine. We remember this scene later when Gudrun and Gerald embrace under the railway-bridge—'how . . . powerful and terrible was his embrace' (Chapter 24, p.373). Taming his mare, Gerald is 'calm as a ray of cold sunshine' and Gudrun is 'calm and cold', 'cold and indifferent' (Chapter 9, p.124); this prepares for the cold mountains of the last chapters and Gudrun's cold indifference when Gerald dies. 'Inter-relatedness' is at work among characters and themes, and in the clusters of imagery and symbolic contrasts which add to the novel's poetry and design.

The style

Style, as we have just seen, is a part of the structure of *Women in Love*. Techniques with a structural purpose do not always succeed in the writing, however. The picture of Birkin as an Egyptian Pharaoh can be connected with African and exotic images elsewhere in the novel, but the passage at the end of Chapter 23 is considered a failure by Lawrence's warmest admirers. The countess at Breadalby is compared to a stoat (few novelists use animals better than Lawrence); when she is compared to a weasel and to a water-rat, a few pages later, the writing seems facile. Lawrence found it easy to write effectively. He sometimes spoils his effects by overdoing them.

Lawrence can be evocative in a few simple words, as in Birkin's picture of the world after man's extinction: 'don't you find it a beautiful clean thought, a world empty of people, just uninterrupted grass, and a hare sitting up?' (Chapter 11, p.142). The unpeopled planet is made vivid by this simple word-picture of a hare in the grasslands. The writing can also be neat and witty: 'Birkin came with Hermione. She had a rapt, triumphant look, like the fallen angels restored, yet still subtly demoniacal' (Chapter 1, p.24). Other images are appropriate: Gerald's mare rears 'as if lifted up on a wind of terror' (Chapter 9, p.123). Birkin, moving among the desks in Ursula's class-room, impresses Ursula: 'his presence was so quiet, almost like a vacancy in the corporate air' (Chapter 3, p.39). The last phrase is surprising and right for the digni- fied stranger in a schoolroom's crowded atmosphere.

Lawrence makes less use of biblical imagery in *Women in Love* than in *The Rainbow*; but here London is a doomed and corrupt city, like Sodom; apocalyptic motifs obsess Birkin's mind; Halliday suggests that Birkin aims to 'harrow' the Pompadour as Christ harrowed Hell. Repetition, parallel phrasing, and sentence rhythm are often reminis- cent of the Bible: 'she was blind, she could see no more. Her soul did not look out' (Chapter 29, p.440, where Ursula is in the train).

Throughout the novel there are good descriptions of scenes and people, usually in copious detail. The Brangwen family, feeling awk- ward as they arrive at Shortlands for the lake-party, go through the gate four-abreast; Will Brangwen is tall and ruddy 'with his narrow boyish brow drawn with irritation'; his wife is 'perfectly collected, though her hair was slipping on one side'; Gudrun, with dark staring eyes and sulky face, seems to be backing away as she advances; and Ursula has 'the odd, brilliant, dazzled look that always came when she was in some false situation' (Chapter 14, p.177). Each is distinctly seen in this moment of slight embarrassment. Ursula's journey to Innsbruck in the opening section of Chapter 29 shows Lawrence's skill as a travel writer: in the channel-boat, the port and railway-station at Ostend, the train full of Belgians with long brown beards, the vaguer impressions of shops in Switzerland as Ursula tires, and the happy arrival in an open sledge over the snow, Lawrence uses just enough detail and no more, and conveys the experience of travel.

In the dialogues we hear the characters: when Hermione is teasing

Birkin in the class-room in Chapter 3, her voice 'sings' and 'grunts' and her assertiveness sounds through her words: 'Do you really think, Rupert . . . do you really think it is worth while? Do you really think the children are better for being roused to consciousness?' (p.43). The repetition of 'really' helps to make the last phrase seem pretentious and silly. Birkin's schoolmasterliness can often be heard: ' "the point about love," he said, "is that we hate the word because we have vulgarised it" ' (Chapter 11, p.145). He is talking to Ursula as if she were a lecture-room. Elsewhere he speaks well, as in his lines about the hare. Many of the characters make earnest, impassioned speeches to each other, but Lawrence knows how conversation veers about: the debate on education in Chapter 8 breaks off when someone remembers an absurd phrase from the book she is reading (p.96). Other speakers are less polished. Will Brangwen's fury at his daughters' laughter on the road to Short-lands is refreshingly plain: 'I'll see if I'm going to be followed by a pair of giggling, yelling jackanapes . . . I'm going back home if there's any more of this . . .' (Chapter 14, p.175). In Chapter 27 he calls Ursula a 'shifty bitch' (p.411). Winifred, as a very young lady reproaching her rabbit with bad manners, sounds just right: 'Bismarck, Bismarck, you are behaving terribly!' (Chapter 18, p.270).

There is no doubt about the success of Lawrence's style in these passages. But there are features of the writing in *Women in Love* which can irritate and distract the reader. Lawrence deliberately developed what he called a 'violent' style in *The Rainbow* and in *Women in Love*. Its most obvious device is remorseless repetition. Hermione's assault on Birkin with the paperweight uses 'ecstasy', 'unutterable', and 'con-summation' so often that the words lose their force; Lawrence risks seeming ridiculous in such 'over-writing' of emotional scenes. His attempt to convey states of intense inner commotion can result in in-coherence: Birkin leaves Ursula at the end of the lake-party 'satisfied and shattered, fulfilled and destroyed' (Chapter 14, p.210). The word 'loins' appears frequently. Lawrence wants to emphasise the appeal of the men's bodies for Ursula and Gudrun, but he resorts to an archaic euphemism, which is often absurd: 'Oh, and the beauty of the subjec-tion of his loins, white and dimly luminous as he climbed over the side of the boat, made her want to die, to die. The beauty of his dim and luminous loins as he climbed into the boat, his back rounded and soft — ah, this was too much for her, too final a vision' (Chapter 14, p.203). Repetition does not help Lawrence, here, to create the effect he wants; 'too final a vision' is too grand for what are, after all, only loins. These characteristics arise, however, from the author's impatience with tame conventionality; he could not have written at all without that.

The characters

Lawrence's main characters attain to heightened states of being, their minds and emotions raised beyond the common level. J.I.M. Stewart comments in *Eight Modern Writers* that 'persons habitually living at such a pitch could not long avoid nervous disintegration' (p.517). Lawrence's people are displayed in scenes of crisis; the calm interludes in their lives are passed over in a few sentences: 'in Beldover, there was both for Ursula and for Gudrun an interval. It seemed to Ursula as if Birkin had gone out of her for the time . . . Gudrun . . . was now almost indifferent . . .' (Chapter 17, p.237). Such intervals do not interest this novelist; he concentrates on storms of emotion in which we see—as Stewart says—'scarcely character in the received acceptation of the term at all' but rather 'forces of the human psyche' (*Eight Modern Writers*, p.518). Lawrence had renounced 'the old stable ego of the character'; in *Women in Love* he aimed to reveal both unconscious drives and forces of nature at work in his characters. Nonetheless, we are reading a story, and we look instinctively for the clues to character which we use in assessing people we know. Some novelists since Lawrence wrote have moved much further away from traditional presentation of personality.

The fact that several of his friends saw themselves in *Women in Love* shows that its characters are recognisable as people and not just 'forces of the human psyche'. Birkin reflects the way the author saw himself, although Birkin is not Lawrence, and Ursula is not Frieda. The presence of historical figures behind *Women in Love* is interesting to social historians; certainly, Lawrence caused pain to friends, though that is not relevant to judgement of the book. He rightly spoke of 'the world of my novel' and his characters belong there.

Birkin

Rupert Birkin is an isolated hero: he seems to have no family; his background is vague. Like Lawrence he is well-educated, intelligent, articulate, argumentative and sensitive. Like Lawrence he is interested in art and botany, in languages and history, but most of all in people. Lawrence was a schoolmaster until 1911; Birkin is a school-inspector. Lawrence longed for a private income; Birkin has four hundred pounds a year of his own, which was enough to live on comfortably sixty years ago. Like Lawrence Birkin is often ill, but remains—periodically—energetic, though more concerned with finding the best way to live than with advancing a career within existing society.

Birkin's ideas can be found in Lawrence's letters and other writings. He detests modern England—ruined, he thinks by a false faith in technological progress. He is often close to despair, at times misanthropic and given to dreaming of the end of the world. He hates cynicism, however, and looks for his own 'salvation' (he has no orthodox religious belief) in an 'ultimate' marriage and a 'sacred' friendship. He hopes in this way to find freedom with responsibility, and he sees the formation of such relationships as the only chance of society's regeneration.

Birkin fears maternal possessiveness (as Lawrence did). He curses the 'Great Mother' goddess of antiquity who, he thinks, lives in all women. He escapes from Hermione's demanding love and tries to convince Ursula that a man's 'self-abandonment' in marriage is wrong. A devoted friendship with another man would apparently help Birkin resist female domination. He loves Gerald, though hating what he stands for, and wants friendship to include physical (but not sexual) intimacy, as it does in the wrestling. He wants to go beyond love, in marriage and in friendship, to achieve an 'equilibrium' between partners who are both committed and free.

Birkin admits to Ursula that he talks like Hamlet, putting off action for the sake of endless speculation. She thinks him like a preacher or Sunday-school teacher. Halliday and his friends deride the pompous, prophetic tone of his language: 'it almost supersedes the Bible—' (Chapter 29, p.432). Lawrence could see his own faults. Nonetheless he is charming, socially skilful though never quite socially relaxed, high-spirited and exuberant at times; he has integrity; he is gentle with children; he loathes the immorality of Halliday and Loerke. We are meant to accept him as a good man—though far from perfect.

Gerald

Gerald Crich is the child of an unsuccessful marriage. He has grown up fearing and avoiding his father; hating school; and dreaming of adventures as a soldier or explorer, as most boys do. He goes on to explore the Amazon and serve in the army. Handsome, athletic, rich, and intelligent, he appears a model English gentleman of the time. His mother thinks him 'wanting', however, and 'weak as a cat' (Chapter 24, p.369). The accident in which he killed his brother in childhood has perhaps unnerved him for life. He lives by will-power. He imposes his will on the miners, introducing efficient new methods. He believes in hard work (which Lawrence, though a hard worker, mistrusted). His recreations are reading (anthropology and philosophy), riding, and talking to

Birkin whom he likes and finds soothing but does not take too seriously. Unmarried, he visits girls in London, and prefers to pay them.

Some readers respect Gerald more than Lawrence intended; some consider him a tragic figure; others think him a victim of the author's scheme for the novel. Birkin calls him, in a phrase which gives the key to his presentation, 'a born unbeliever' (Chapter 5, p.64). He wants power and sensual pleasure, and finds both with Gudrun; but he does not believe in the sanctity of life and love as Birkin does. He depends on Gudrun as a comforting mother-figure, but fails to create a true understanding with her. Unbelieving, he is insecure; several scenes imply that his insecurity makes him cruel; he can be violent, as we see at the end.

Lawrence uses imagery, more than psychology, to express his nature. He is bright, white, cold, and northern, like the Arctic or like the Austrian mountains where he dies. His background and his way of life have frozen his nature so that he cannot love Gudrun or Birkin. Lawrence means his death to represent the failure of the industrious but insensitive English ruling-class to which he belongs.

Ursula

Ursula Brangwen's career as a teacher has made her independent; she loves her father but will not be 'bullied' by him, or by anyone else. She dislikes Hermione's condescension. Like her sister she fears routine domesticity. She expects to be allowed to follow her own feelings. She has had lovers (including Skrebensky of *The Rainbow* whom she often thinks of and refers to); she considers herself superior and expects a superior husband.

She is sensitive and protective—menacing Birkin with her motherliness. She believes in love and resents Birkin's lectures on the subject and his hopes for something beyond. She is jealous of Hermione and uneasy about Birkin's love for Gerald. She can be wilful; she leaves Gudrun behind when Birkin invites them both to tea; and she announces her wedding, at home, the night before. Her moods, her brooding on death, her depression over home life and school routine, her occasional petulance, all seem very normal. She calls herself a 'rose of happiness' (Chapter 14, p.193); she has a capacity for joy and love which heartens and revives Birkin. She is milder, calmer and more delicate than her sister. Having lived in Beldover while Gudrun was in London she is more accustomed to the squalor of local conditions and more able to put up with people. She has a quick sympathy for Gerald's mare and the stray cat at Birkin's; she respects the integrity of the robin which Gudrun compares to Lloyd George. She is impressionable, adopting some, at least, of Birkin's views, soon after marriage. She is a free spirit, but a 'born wife' despite her independence. The Lawrences' marriage was more quarrelsome than the Birkins's; Ursula is, perhaps, an idealised version of Frieda.

Gudrun

Gudrun's bright clothes and brilliant stockings are a challenge to Beldover. Her exceptional beauty and the success of her tiny wood-carvings in London have helped to make her self-conscious, proud and defensive. Her independence is more aggressive than Ursula's. She envies men their freedom and says so when the sisters are watching Gerald diving; this grows into a resentment and dislike of men, although she is attracted to them. She dislikes and is drawn to the mining community in the same way. She is restless and plans to go abroad. She is gentle and tactful with Winifred and Mr Crich, winning the child's love and the old man's affection; but she is *cold* like Gerald, and like him an 'unbeliever', detached and easily disillusioned. She is unmoved by death, wearing her colourful clothes when the Crich family is in mourning, and unmoved when Gerald dies. Her nature is, as Lawrence said of modern life, 'all split up'.

Like Hermione and Gerald she has a firm will. She takes charge of the situation in the Pompadour, capturing Birkin's letter in his enemies' stronghold. She likes to attract and to exercise power—as when she dances defiantly before the cattle. Her sensuality is connected with a streak of perversity; she is thrilled by Gerald's ruthlessness with animals, but this kind of excitement cannot develop into a lasting relationship. Gudrun is a natural mistress, not a wife. The cynical, morbid, unhealthy Loerke, who is tired of women, appeals to her as a change from Gerald and a means to torment him. Like Gerald, she represents for Lawrence an individual of remarkable abilities who has not learned to live properly. The same can be said of Hermione.

Hermione

The sisters come from the lower middle class although they have become almost classless, as talented girls can. Hermione Roddice belongs to the upper class: she is a baronet's daughter; she receives her guests at her father's Georgian country house; her brother is a Member of Parliament. She is educated and clever, at home in Oxford and Florence. She shares with Birkin a cosmopolitan culture from which

Ursula, depite her schoolteacher's knowledgeability, is excluded. She has adopted the role of a leader of the world of the arts; her voice sings and drawls; she dresses splendidly but oddly. Gudrun's art is being talked about and she therefore has the sisters to Breadalby, enjoying the social daring of inviting girls whose father is not a gentleman. Her views on all subjects are 'advanced'; she echoes Birkin, annoying him.

Hermione is another example of Lawrence's view that insecurity and over-developed will-power go together. Hermione needs Birkin: 'when he was there, she felt complete, she was sufficient, whole. For the rest of the time she was established on the sand' (Chapter 1, p.18). She shores up her insufficiency with culture, vainly, and wants to have Birkin 'safe' at Breadalby. She domineers over everyone and especially over Birkin. The incident of the rug in Chapter 12 is significant: she makes a claim on him with an expensive present. Birkin rebels against her when he meets Ursula, and she finds a kind of 'consummation' in a violent act. Ursula is jealous of her; she tries to dominate and discourage Ursula. She disappears from the novel when no longer needed for her effect on Birkin and Ursula, after Chapter 23.

Mr Crich

Mr Thomas Crich is a Christian gentleman. He has been a patriarchal Victorian colliery-owner, presiding over his wife and family, his workers, and the four mining towns of the district, with charitable care. He has regarded all as his fellow Christians—disciplining his children, in spite of his wife's objections; and dispensing money to the poorest of his neighbours, to his wife's fury. The miners have done well; 'having a sufficient fortune [Mr Crich] thought only of the men . . . There were few poor and few needy' (Chapter 17, p.252). But this has led to discontent and to strikes which have 'broken his heart'. He has given up control of the mines to Gerald. Now he faces the 'darkness' of his approaching death. He respects his wife with a distant, pure love (from which she retreats); his children have grown up nervous of him; Lawrence insists that the father's Christianity has a chilling effect on his family. He is left with his love for Winifred, arranging for Gudrun to take charge of her and save her from the rigours of school. To Gerald, watching Mr Crich die, 'the whole unifying idea of mankind seemed to be dying with his father' (Chapter 17, p.248). The Industrial Magnate has represented a social order, inadequate and misguided, Lawrence thinks, but powerful and well-meaning nonetheless. Mr Crich will have no successor.

Mrs Crich

Gerald's mother is a vague, withdrawn figure, who has given up her fight against her husband's resolute philanthropy and now 'like a hawk in a cage' has 'sunk into silence' (p.242). Her husband has loved her but not understood her; she has given him many children but regarded herself as his prisoner. She still resents him when his body is laid out looking younger in death, because she feels he has robbed her of life. Although only dimly aware of the world she can see the weakness in Gerald, perhaps by contrast with her masterful husband. Rude and crazy, wandering the countryside, staring keenly and seeing nothing, she is perhaps a more 'tragic' figure than Gerald.

Will Brangwen

The sisters exasperate their father, Will. Ursula infuriates him when she refuses to be 'bullied' into marrying Birkin, and when she announces that she has decided to marry him next day. Gudrun's clothes are 'a sore trial' to her father on the day of the party at Shortlands (Chapter 8, p.174), and so is the up-to-date independence of both his daughters. A school handicraft instructor, he is shy and awkward when he goes to Shortlands. He tells Birkin, in Chapter 19, that Ursula 'has had everything that's right for a girl to have' for a good upbringing, and he hopes that 'new-fangled ways' won't spoil her. Birkin bewilders him.

Mrs Brangwen

Their mother seems to the sisters like a stately baroness: she is shabby and untidy, but unaware of it; she walks demurely and wears her clothes with perfect ease and satisfaction. Like the colliery people who feel 'as if this catastrophe had happened directly to themselves' (Chapter 14, p.213) she sympathises with the family at Shortlands when Diana is drowned, and resents Birkin's criticism of them. She is hurt by the quarrels between Ursula and Will, but writes to Ursula after her marriage although Will Brangwen does not.

Winifred

At thirteen Winifred is fond of her father and devoted to her pets, marvelling at them and crooning to them. She is pleased that Gudrun is to be a friend, not a servant; this is a novelty. Her gravity and excitement, when Gudrun returns to Shortlands in Chapter 21 and she presents her bouquet, amuse her father and Gerald (whom she likes because he is self-contained). Lawrence was keenly aware of children; the character of Winifred is one of the most pleasing minor features of the novel.

Halliday

A young artist with a 'rather degenerate face' and 'no mind' (according to his mistress), Halliday represents a wealthy but unstable type of Londoner living in an underworld of second-rate artists, musicians and intellectuals. He is morally lost. 'Julius', says Birkin, 'is somewhat insane. On the one hand he's had religious mania, and on the other, he is fascinated by obscenity' (Chapter 8, p.106). Lawrence's enemies might have said this of him in 1916; perhaps in creating Halliday he was asserting his own—as well as Birkin's—good sense and morality. Halliday does serve as a foil to Birkin; he is shown to be ridiculous and pathetic in Chapters 6 and 7, then made to ridicule Birkin in Chapter 28.

Minette

Minette is beautiful, with 'round blue eyes like stagnant, unhappy pools' (Chapter 7, p.88); she seems to Gerald like a slave-girl, which at first excites, later disgusts him. She has been Halliday's mistress but he has sent her away—pregnant—to the country. Lawrence succeeds, in Chapters 6 and 7 and 28, in convincing the reader that she is without any personality; she acts her part, sadly, in the shadowy café. Her name is meant to recall the other underworld of the mines.

Loerke

Herr Loerke is gruesome. Wretched but stoical, he lives only for his art. A conversation in Chapter 29 reveals him completely. He is telling Gudrun how the girl who served as model for his Lady Godiva would not keep still: 'I slapped her hard . . . then she'd sit for five minutes'. He beat her, he admits 'nonchalantly', harder than he ever 'beat anything'. 'I had to. It was the only way I got the work done'. Gudrun asks why he chose such a young Godiva. He says he doesn't 'like them any bigger'. After eighteen, girls are no good to him. 'They are no good to me, they are of no use in my art' he repeats impatiently (pp.487-8). In men he likes 'stupid form'. Otherwise people mean little to him, though he prides himself on understanding women better than Gerald can.

Part 4

Hints for study

Study topics

These topics are related to the earlier parts of these Notes.

Introduction

(1) How did Lawrence's parents influence his early life?
(2) What results of Lawrence's years as a schoolmaster can you see in *Women in Love*?
(3) Lawrence grew up in a mining village; how did this affect his attitude to English society?
(4) Why did Lawrence want to leave England?
(5) What did Lawrence think of the effects of industrial development in England during the nineteenth century?
(6) Did these changes improve conditions of life for people like Lawrence?
(7) Which writers most influenced him and why? What shortcomings did he see in earlier novelists?

Summaries

(1) List the main incidents of the novel in order.
(2) Make a list of scenes (*a*) involving two people (*b*) involving a group of people.
(3) Trace the progress (*a*) of Ursula's relationship with Birkin (*b*) of Gudrun's relationship with Gerald.
(4) Trace the progress of Hermione's relationship with Birkin.
(5) Make a list of turning-points in the story (for example, Hermione's assault on Birkin at Breadalby). Show what happens as a result in each case.
(6) Summarise in your own words some of the major scenes: the wedding in the first chapter; Hermione's house-party at Breadalby; the water-party, and so on.

Commentary

Nature, purpose and achievement
(1) What was Lawrence's attitude to his novel when he had finished it?
(2) What makes it an original novel?
(3) What makes it traditional?
(4) What was Lawrence's reaction to the First World War?
(5) How did he regard the state of England in 1916?
(6) What is the significance of marriage in *Women in Love*? What is Birkin's view of marriage? How does this relate to Lawrence's ideas about modern society?
(7) Why did critics object to Lawrence's work?
(8) What was his attitude to censorship?
(9) What was his approach to characterisation?

Structure
(1) How is it possible to compare a novel's structure to that of a dramatic poem?
(2) What kinds of pattern can be found in *Women in Love*?
(3) How does Lawrence organise his group of characters?
(4) How does Lawrence use Hermione to advance the relationship of Birkin and Ursula?
(5) In what sense do Birkin and Ursula succeed where Gerald and Gudrun fail?
(6) Make lists of different types of contrast: between characters, groups, settings, scenes.
(7) What advantage does the novel gain from the change of scene to Austria?
(8) How are the novel's themes connected with relationships among the characters?
(9) What is the meaning of 'pattern' in fiction? What kinds of pattern can be found in *Women in Love*?
(10) What is the significance of the deaths in the Crich family?
(11) What use does Lawrence make of symbolism?
(12) List images of darkness, of light, of coldness, of 'the underworld'.
(13) How does Lawrence prepare for the mountain setting of the last three chapters?

Style
(1) Find examples of good descriptive writing in *Women in Love*.
(2) Make a list of images which seem effective. Why are they effective?
(3) What makes good dialogue?

(4) If you were given passages of dialogue without the characters' names, could you identify them? Test yourself with the following extracts and explain how you can identify the speakers by the way they talk:

' "There's the whole difference in the world," he said, "between the actual sensual being and the vicious mental deliberate profligacy our lot goes in for. In our night-time, there's always the electricity switched on, we watch ourselves, we get it all in the head, really." '

'Salsie, won't you play something? Won't somebody dance? Gudrun, you will dance, won't you? I wish you would. *Anche tu, Palestra . . .*? [And you, Palestra?] You too, Ursula.'

'He scratches most awfully sometimes. Oh, do look at him, isn't he wonderful! Bismarck! How *dreadful* you are! You are beastly '

'Don't you think you might as well get yourself up for a Christmas cracker, an' ha' done with it?'

(5) Look closely at Halliday's reading of Birkin's letter in Chapter 28, p.433. Why do the phrases amuse Halliday? Does Birkin talk like this?

(6) Do you think that Lawrence sometimes 'overwrites'? What does this term mean?

(7) Find examples of repetition (*a*) of words (*b*) of phrases. Are they successful?

(8) Make a list of words which seem both surprising and appropriate in their context.

(9) Study Lawrence's use of detail in describing: faces; gestures; clothes; houses; landscape.

Characters

(1) Contrast, point by point: Birkin and Gerald;
Ursula and Gudrun;
Ursula and Hermione;
Birkin and Halliday;
Gudrun and Minette;
Gerald and Mr Crich;
Birkin and Ursula.

Compare, point by point: Ursula and Gudrun;
Gerald and Gudrun;
Gerald and Hermione;
Birkin and Lawrence.

(2) Imagine that you are to advise the actors in a dramatised version of *Women in Love*. What advice would you give to each player?

(3) What scenes would you choose to bring out what each of the characters is like? Why?

(4) How does Lawrence try to influence the way the reader thinks about the characters?

(5) How do Lawrence's people differ from characters in other novels you know well? Are his characters distinct from each other? Are we liable to confuse any of them? Are we liable to forget any of them? Are we likely to remember them long after reading the novel?

Patterns and themes

Here are some groups of topics and points to concentrate on:

THEMES:	marriage	work
	'life'	'coldness'; instrumentality
	culture	industrialism
	sensuality	abstraction
	spontaneity	will-power
	love	death
MOTIFS:	the countryside	the mines
	Africa	the North
	art	technology
	animals	machines
	'rebirth'	destruction, and the end of the world
SETTINGS:	England	Austria
	London	the Midlands
	the Pompadour	Beldover
	Breadalby	Birkin's mill
	Shortlands	the mines

Quotations for illustration

Students should form the habit of finding apt quotations for use in essays and examination answers. Brief quotations from the novel appear throughout Part 3 of these Notes. Look for others, and be careful to study the context in which the words appear. Comments often reveal the speaker: when Hermione says that Birkin is 'like a boy who must pull everything to pieces to see how it is made' (Chapter 12, p.158), we learn about her, not him. She shows her urge to dominate him, in calling him a boy (she calls him 'a sulky boy' at Breadalby in Chapter 8) and in trying to contain him in a formula. Although Birkin wants to understand things, he believes in wholeness. What he tells Hermione about the drawing of Chinese geese, in Chapter 8, could be used here.

Look for brief quotations with many implications. When Birkin calls Gerald 'a born unbeliever' (Chapter 5, p.64), the words provide a key to Birkin's earnestness and to his view of Gerald. They prepare for the cynicism of Halliday's circle in the next chapter, and relate to the novel's nature and purpose: Birkin, like Lawrence, believes in belief, although it is hard for him to find his own. When Gerald says, in the same chapter, that his life has been 'making things *go*' (p.63), his words can be connected with the sisters' discussion of his '*go*' (his energy) in the previous chapter; 'things' implies the 'machine' of Chapter 17, and his neglect of human values. When Halliday jokingly tells Minette that Birkin thinks her a 'flower of mud' (Chapter 28, p.433), the phrase conveys Halliday's cynical treatment of her and Birkin's view of her sorry situation; it recalls images of flowers throughout the novel.

Here are a few quotations. Look up their contexts:

BIRKIN AND URSULA:
'There was something in his presence, Ursula thought, lambent and alive' (Chapter 27, p.423)

'"I was becoming quite dead-alive, nothing but a word-bag," he said in triumph.' (Chapter 14, p.210)

'"Aren't I enough for you?" she asked. "No," he said. "You are enough for me, as far as a woman is concerned."' (Chapter 31, p.541)

GERALD AND GUDRUN:
'He saw her a dangerous, hostile spirit, that could stand undiminished . . .' (Chapter 10, p.135)

'He had all his life been tortured by a furious and destructive demon.' (Chapter 17, p.257)

'My God! this was a barren tragedy, barren, barren.' (Chapter 31, p.535)

BIRKIN AND GERALD:
'Gerald really loved Birkin, though he never quite believed in him.' (Chapter 16, p.226)

HERMIONE:
'She was a woman of the new school, full of intellectuality, and heavy, nerve-worn with consciousness . . . there was a terrible void . . . within her.' (Chapter 1, pp.17–18)

THE SETTING:
'They turned off the main road, past a black patch of common-garden, where sooty cabbage stumps stood shameless.' (Chapter 1, p.12)

'She looked round, and saw peak beyond peak of rock and snow, bluish, transcendent in heaven.' (Chapter 29, p.472)

Arranging material

Two hints should always be kept in mind: to distinguish between the essential and the incidental; and to view the novel as a whole—its overall design and meaning, whatever topic is undertaken in an essay or answer.

Suppose, for example, you are writing about the character of Birkin. Details such as his job as a school-inspector or his four hundred pounds a year can be kept in reserve: do not start with these. Look for some idea about him which will allow you to organise an answer; you might begin by saying that Birkin is a natural teacher. This is one way of regarding him and it gives us a method for proceeding. His professional concern with teaching (as an inspector), his education, culture and articulacy, his interest in art and botany, and his tenderness with children, can be discussed in terms of his profession. We can point out how he resembles Lawrence, who worked as a schoolmaster until 1911. The scene in Ursula's class-room in Chapter 3 shows us Birkin, briefly, at work; he is beginning to take over the lesson, sending away for crayons to colour the drawings of catkins, when Hermione interrupts. However theoretical his approach to life and love, he can be attentive to practical details.

Developing this idea, we can consider the didacticism of his manner and speech, and his earnestness of mind. He lectures other people. 'The point about love . . .' he begins when courting Ursula (in Chapter 11, p.145). He has the teacher's habit of talking too much; he calls himself 'a word-bag' (in Chapter 14, p.210). There is a primness and self-righteousness about him which remind Ursula of a Sunday-school teacher, and remind Halliday of a clergyman or a Biblical prophet. These are symptoms of his sincerity, which reflects the author's commitment to taking life seriously. Discovering his ideal of equilibrium in marriage and friendship matters more to Birkin than his job. He gives that up when Ursula accepts him.

We could go on to discuss his relationships with Hermione, Gerald and Ursula. We see him instructing Hermione even in moments of intense emotional strain. His love for Gerald is partly a wish to convert him to healthier views; he acts as Gerald's moral tutor, in the train, for example, and at Breadalby. Ursula is his ideal pupil; by the end of the novel she is trying to coach Gudrun in his ideas.

Here you have a brief illustration (which could be filled out and extended) of how a straightforward topic can be managed. First, look for what seems to you essential in the question set; perhaps that the novel is dramatic, or that Gerald's story is a tragedy, or that the method is one of contrast, or that Lawrence is always concerned with values. Follow your own judgement, and try to apply your judgement to the requirements of the answer, choosing an idea which will connect together the incidental points you want to make. It is better to be bold and clear, in an examination especially, even at the cost of simplifying.

In using detail try to make each point serve a purpose. Quotations should be used to illustrate points. Do not make excessive use of quotation, though, and do not quote just for the sake of it.

Specimen questions

Questions could be set on all the topics treated in the Commentary and on others suggested in these Hints for study. Students should look carefully at the precise wording of a question.

Major topics

(1) Examine the theme of marriage in *Women in Love*.
(2) How does Lawrence use his settings?
(3) Comment on Gerald's death as an ending for the novel.
(4) Write on the presentation of women in the novel. How well does Lawrence understand women?
(5) Discuss Lawrence's treatment of dialogue, or description, or symbolism.
(6) In what ways can we talk of the writer's 'poetic imagination' in *Women in Love*?
(7) Show how characters are contrasted and explain why.
(8) Explain the purposes behind one of the following scenes: Hermione's assault on Birkin at Breadalby; Birkin stoning the moon's reflection; Gudrun in the Pompadour.
(9) Does the novel create a full and convincing picture of a social world?
(10) How do the sisters differ?
(11) Outline Birkin's ideas about modern English society.
(12) What is Hermione's role in the novel?
(13) Write on Lawrence as a satirist in *Women in Love*.
(14) Write on education in *Women in Love*.

Minor topics

---

(1) Write on one of the following: the visual arts, children, animals, the mines, the world of nature, in *Women in Love*.
(2) Illustrate Lawrence's use of costume.
(3) What is the role of Loerke?
(4) What is the role of Minette?
(5) Explain Ursula's attitude to her father.
(6) How does Gerald differ from his father?
(7) What is the purpose of the wrestling scene?
(8) Comment on the scene of the chair.

Specimen answers

Major topics, *Question (1):* Examine the theme of marriage in *Women in Love*.

Women in Love begins with two girls questioning marriage; the novel is concerned with the whole social context of their doubts. Ursula and Gudrun can afford to question. They are financially independent, and willing to take lovers. For such 'advanced' young women in 1916, marriage was ceasing to govern all relations between the sexes. The implications of that are considered in *Women in Love*.

The Crich and Brangwen parents have lived in a world that took marriage for granted as a sacred and permanent institution. Will Brangwen tells Birkin that 'it's no good looking round afterwards, when it's too late' (Chapter 19, p.289). Birkin's reply that 'if one repents being married, the marriage is at an end' disconcerts him and he starts to talk about Ursula's proper upbringing. He is understandably angry when Ursula treats her wedding as a private, not a family affair. Although the sisters scoff at their parents' domesticity, and although Birkin thinks Will 'uncreated' and in no real sense Ursula's parent (p.288), many readers feel that Ursula and Gudrun have gained from the security of an old-fashioned family. Gerald, however, is the child of an unsuccessful marriage. Mrs Crich has fought against her husband with the spirit of a demon; and, firm in the sense of his own justice and her purity, he has failed to notice. For her, Victorian marriage has been 'a cage'. Lawrence writes of the Criches' 'relation of utter inter-destruction' (Chapter 17, p.244), which has drained his vitality and almost destroyed her reason.

The image of marriage as a trap appears elsewhere. ' 'Slike when you're dead,' says the girl who is given the chair; 'you're a long time married'

(Chapters 26, p.406). Her young man shudders, though he seems re-signed to the prospect. He has no chance of escape: the girl is pregnant; they are poor. We recall Birkin's words to Gerald in the previous chapter: 'marriage in the old sense seems to me repulsive . . . it's a sort of tacit hunting in couples: the world is all in couples, each couple in its own little house, watching its own little interests, and stewing in its own little privacy—it's the most repulsive thing on earth'. Gerald agrees that 'there's something inferior about it' (Chapter 25, p.397). Birkin's dis-taste is linked with his objection to living only for material well-being, expressed in their earlier discussion in the train in Chapter 5. Town life in Lawrence's time was beginning to isolate couples and produce what Birkin calls *égoïsme à deux* ('selfish units of two') more cut off from the community than the Brangwens and Criches have been. Gerald and the sisters share something of Birkin's 'repulsion'.

Gudrun calls marriage 'a social arrangem. nt' which has nothing to do with the question of love. Two people may be in love for the whole of their lives '—perhaps. But marriage is neither here nor there, even then' (Chapter 21, p.326). There is nothing traditionally sacred to her about the 'arrangement' and she thinks Birkin's belief in a sacred mar-riage 'rather vague' (p.327). A mistress, she tells Gerald, is more likely to be faithful than a wife; she becomes his mistress and rejects him. Many writers of the time (including Thomas Hardy) had given cur-rency to the ideas Gudrun airs here. Halliday and his circle are familiar with them; richer and more lax in behaviour than Gudrun is, they are even further removed from the values that belonged to traditional marriage.

In Gerald and Gudrun we see dissatisfaction with 'marriage in the old sense'; and nothing to replace it. Birkin dreams of a life adventur-ously shared between partners fully aware of each other—which might as well be marriage. At times he hopes that the world's salvation may lie in such relationships; but he dreads being trapped, even by Ursula, and asks her, 'Does it end with just our two selves?' (Chapter 26, p.409). On the last page he tells Ursula that she is not enough for him. Their relationship has succeeded, but Birkin is too angry with society to feel comfortable as a mere husband. Happily Ursula is capable of calming him: 'while we are only people' she tells him, 'we've got to take the world that's given' (Chapter 23, p.355), and marriage, she believes, is given too.

Women in Love conveys the doubts of its time about marriage and about the social stability which it had once represented to everyone. Birkin and Gerald have the money and leisure to be troubled by such questions, and the sisters are exceptional in the social freedom with which they have to come to terms; most girls in 1916 would have envied them. Higher education was presenting young women with such opportunities and problems for the first time. The sisters and their lovers are 'advanced'; two generations later, their debate about marriage and society can still seem up to date.

Question (2): How does Lawrence use his settings?

Lawrence, like Birkin, wants to explain the state of the whole world, but his novel is set in the areas and social circles he knew best. The convincing background lends reality to his characters, and contributes a depth to the symbolism and poetry of the novel. Accepting the settings, the reader is involved in everything else.

Lawrence had used his own region of Nottinghamshire in his earlier novels. He had already gained a reputation, even among critics reluctant to praise him, for his power to bring to life the part of England he knew best. He liked to put the neighbourhood of Eastwood into his fiction. Lamb Close House and its reservoir, which belonged to a mine-owner not far from Eastwood, became Shortlands and Willey Water in *Women in Love*. Lamb Close, like Shortlands, was a rebuilt farm; to the north was a Willey Spring. Lawrence knew how the smoke from the mines would be visible from their owner's country house. He knew even better the miners' dwellings of blackened brick and slate, the black paths, iron fences and stile 'rubbed shiny by the moleskins of the passing miners' (Chapter 1, p.12). The scenes which frighten Gudrun when she comes home to Beldover are based on Eastwood. Breadalby, in the Derbyshire hills, with its pillars and quiet lawns, far from the mining 'underworld', owes much to Lawrence's visits to Garsington Manor near Oxford. The secluded calm and beauty of Breadalby is juxtaposed with the slate villages of the next chapter, 'Coal dust'; and the formal life of the great houses is contrasted with the glittering smoke-filled Pompadour café (suggested by the Café Royal in London). These English scenes of green and black (words often repeated) are opposed to the white mountains of the Austrian Tyrol, which Lawrence had visited in 1912: 'a white perfect cradle of snow, new and frozen, sweeping up on either side, black crags and white sweeps of silver towards the pale blue heavens' (Chapter 29, p.447). The various settings of the book are always visually convincing.

Lawrence peoples his settings. We see the women, 'arms folded over their coarse aprons', staring at the sisters in Chapter 1 (p.12), and hear their voices—'What price the stockings!' (p.14)—and those of the workmen of 'Coal dust' and the miner who guides Gerald to the Brangwens' house in Chapter 25. The minor characters and background figures are vivid and appropriate. The guests at Breadalby, the Pompadour drinkers and the Continental tourists of the last chapters give the novel a crowded, realistic background. Some of these figures have acquired traits from people Lawrence knew—Bertrand Russell (Sir Joshua) and the mistress of his friend Philip Heseltine (Minette).

The settings inspire confidence and help Lawrence bring his major characters to life. Birkin's moods, dreams, and lectures sometimes seem fantastic but they belong to a man who tramps to Beldover to propose to Ursula, and although its 'straight, final streets' (Chapter 19, p.287) look to him 'like Jerusalem', the reader believes in him against that sure background. The characters are often presented through their response to settings: the sisters arriving at Breadalby, impressed but determined not to be over-impressed; Birkin suffering as his train enters London; Ursula 'strangled' by the harsh brilliance of the mountains.

A character's relation to the background can also help to explain him. As a Crich, Gerald is a public figure in the towns the family owns. When Diana is drowned, there is a 'hush of dreadful excitement' and 'the colliery people . . . were more shocked and frightened than if their own men had been killed. Such a tragedy in Shortlands, the high home of the district' (Chapter 14, p.212). The young Lawrence had watched from a distance the heir of Lamb Court House riding squire-like on his lands (and, once, controlling his horse at a railway crossing). Gerald's social position and inner loneliness are linked, for Lawrence; Gerald is raised above the people among whom Ursula and Gudrun move.

The novel's symbols of darkness: dark waters, dark country—and light: white skin, white mountains—are strengthened by the contrasts in the background. Mines and mountains have a symbolic force, and descriptive passages result in complex patterns of the key-words on which Lawrence's style often depends. 'Still the faint glamour of blackness persisted over the fields and the wooded hills, and seemed darkly to gleam in the air' (Chapter 1, p.13); this is good description, but it also contributes to the novel's view of a sullied world, and to the meaning of many reiterated words: 'corruption', 'devilish', 'violation'. Lawrence relies on his settings throughout.

Question (3): Comment on Gerald's death as an ending for the novel.

Gerald is doomed. Like Cain, he has killed his brother. Catastrophe pursues him; at his happiest moment with Gudrun, his sister falls into the lake and is drowned, killing—ominously—her rescuer. Birkin foresees Gerald's death: 'was he fated to pass away in this knowledge, this one process of frost-knowledge, death by perfect cold? Was he a messenger, an omen of the universal dissolution into whiteness and snow?' (Chapter 19, p.287). Lawrence has prepared for Gerald's death in the mountains. Some critics see his end as tragic; others think it contrived for the sake of the novel's scheme.

Whenever a major character in fiction dies young and unhappy, critics are likely to call him tragic. The term belongs strictly to the theatre. The tragic heroes of Shakespeare are great men who perish through a fault in character and leave us with a sense of awe. The case for Gerald as a tragic hero can be made on these lines. He is a remarkable man: talented, urbane, industrious, strong-willed, practical, and very charming; an athlete, administrator, traveller, soldier and intellectual. He possesses, too, a quality or promise which Birkin values: in Lawrence's terms, a 'gleam of life' which is never fulfilled. Gazing at his dead friend, Birkin tells Ursula 'it is a bitter thing to me' (Chapter 31, p.540). Gerald perishes because he cannot love Birkin or Gudrun well enough; he is 'cold' within. Since he is made so (partly) by industrialised modernity, he is—though not the king or general of tragic drama—a representative figure. His tragedy, it can be argued, is that of the English ruling class which has his merits and limitations. Some readers, however, will feel that Gerald lacks the grandeur of tragedy. Others will be too conscious of Lawrence's design to accept the illusion of a fine man destroyed from within.

J.I.M. Stewart, in *Eight Modern Writers*, says of Gerald that 'from early on we cannot help feeling that Lawrence has created him to have, so to speak, the raw end of the thesis. This is perhaps the grand weakness of *Women in Love*' (p.524). Gerald represents will-power, work for its own sake, mechanical efficiency, sensuality without love, dependence on a mother-substitute, and acceptance of existing social conventions: these are all deadly, in Birkin's mind and the author's. By rejecting blood-brotherhood with Birkin, Gerald has refused his salvation and cannot hope to succeed with Gudrun. Lawrence considered keeping him alive to give Gudrun a son and extend the story, but his thesis, and symbols of cold and death, require Gerald to perish as he does.

Readers will decide these questions for themselves, and consider others. The rejected blood-brotherhood which Birkin regrets, as he contemplates the frozen body in the last chapter, is perhaps a weakness which affects the ending because the novel fails to make clear just what it means. A suppressed Prologue to *Women in Love* implies a more erotic bond than the finished text admits to. Birkin and Gerald holiday in the Tyrol: 'each looked towards the other, and knew the trembling nearness'. Even without the Prologue, it is possible to sympathise with

Gerald's hesitation, and so fail to read the last pages as Lawrence intended.

Nonetheless, the final chapters are powerful and moving. Gerald's despair and suffering as he is tormented by Gudrun's flirtation with Loerke lead to the violent scene which sends him to his death. There is a strong simplicity in the novel's ending. As Gudrun rejects Gerald, the cold white mountains claim him. Lawrence succeeds in conveying the shock of a death among the survivors: the indifferent Gudrun; the futile Loerke; and the Birkins, whose relationship at the close is left unsettled.

Minor topics, *Question (1):* Write on the visual arts in *Women in Love.*

Lawrence was a painter; his interest in the arts affected his view of life. The characters in *Women in Love* are aware of the visual arts: Gudrun sketches and carves; Ursula embroiders; Birkin draws; Halliday paints, and Loerke sculpts. Sculpture, especially, helps to clarify ideas.

Gerald contemplates a statuette from the South Seas in Halliday's flat: a native woman in labour, which he thinks obscene but 'rather wonderful, conveying the suggestion of the extreme of physical sensation, beyond the limits of mental consciousness' (Chapter 6, p.82). The next day he sees Minette in the sculpture; she too is sensual, wonderful, and obscene. Birkin praises the statue which means to him a 'pure culture of sensation', and later he remembers an African carving of Halliday's, elegant but, he thinks, 'purely sensual, purely unspiritual' (Chapter 19, p.285). However wrong-headed Birkin's thoughts about African culture in this passage, the statuette helps him to abandon his creed of sensuality in favour of a higher 'communion' with Ursula. He and Gerald use these sculptures to resolve their relationships: Gerald rejects Minette; Birkin proposes to Ursula.

Gudrun's wood-carvings intrigue the other characters, who wonder if her preoccupation with very small figures gives a clue to what she is like. Ursula tells Hermione that her sister 'must always work small things, that one can put between one's hands . . . She likes to look through the wrong end of the opera-glasses, and see the world that way' (Chapter 3, p.42). Ursula hates subtleties and thinks them a sign of weakness. A limitation in Gudrun and a difference in temperament between the sisters are hinted at here. Discussing the tiny carvings, Ursula talks about mice and lions; her thoughts turn from art to real life.

The question of art and life arises towards the end. Ursula thinks Loerke's horse, bearing Lady Godiva in his bronze sculpture, stiff and unhorselike. 'Horses are sensitive, quite delicate and sensitive really' (Chapter 29, p.483). Loerke treats her as a simpleton: the horse is 'a piece of *form*—'it has no relation to anything outside that work of art'. She retaliates: the stiffness comes from Loerke's own nature. Gudrun defends his view: 'I and my art have nothing to do with each other', she asserts (p.484). Loerke is not alive at all, in Lawrence's sense of the word. Gudrun is wrong. 'The world of art is only the truth about the real world', Ursula tells them (p.485). Lawrence is incidentally contradicting his friend the artist Mark Gertler (1892–1939), but he is showing Ursula's commitment to life and Gudrun's retreat from it. Here, as in several scenes, reactions to works of art bring out the characters and their ideas.

Question (2): Illustrate Lawrence's use of costume.

Costumes in *Women in Love* show Lawrence's pleasure in visual detail and his sense of drama. His characters express themselves in the way they dress.

Gudrun asserts herself with brilliant stockings and clashes of colours. In grass-green stockings, green hat and strong blue coat, she defies the grey colliery town which frightens her. At the water-party she wears pink stockings and a pink, yellow, and black outfit, looking like a fashionable painting, or—her father thinks—like a Christmas cracker. At Shortlands with Winifred she wears blue with woollen yellow stockings, looking like an old-fashioned schoolboy. Legs had been strictly covered up in the nineteenth century. Ursula says 'one gets the greatest joy of all out of really lovely stockings' (Chapter 29, p.491). For both girls, stockings are a badge of emancipation.

Hermione keeps up her reputation with her dress. She is 'the most remarkable woman in the Midlands' (Chapter 1, p.17), and she goes to the Crich wedding in a huge hat with ostrich feathers: 'she was impressive, in her lovely pale-yellow and brownish-rose, yet macabre, something repulsive. People were silent when she passed, impressed, roused, wanting to jeer, yet for some reason silenced' (p.16). At Breadalby her dress is shabby and soiled. Lawrence was (unkindly) satirising the eccentricities of Lady Ottoline Morrell, but the unhappy grandeur of Hermione is appropriately reflected in her costume.

While Gerald is smartly turned out, Birkin, though correctly dressed at the wedding, is made to look slightly ridiculous by an 'innate incongruity' (p.22): he cannot be quite at ease on a formal, conventional occasion. Mrs Brangwen's 'rather odd . . . slip-shod' clothes—black and purple stripes for the water-party—are worn with 'perfect ease and satisfaction' (Chapter 14, p.175); she never doubts herself. Will Brangwen looks 'rather crumped in his best suit' (p.174) and is greeted by

Gerald 'as if he were *not* a gentleman'. Costume was more flamboyant then than now, and held more social meaning. Lawrence was alive to the aesthetic, social and human interest of clothes.

There can be few serious novels in which the characters are more often undressed. Birkin rolls naked among the flowers; he and Gerald strip for their wrestling bout; the sisters bathe naked; nudity is common-place at Halliday's; Birkin dreams of going to a country where clothes aren't needed; Gudrun observes the miners washing after work with their moleskins sliding off. A comment on Gerald helps to explain this feature of *Women in Love*: 'he wanted to keep certain illusions, certain ideas like clothing'. Lawrence disapproves. The body is to be accepted as fully as the 'man—and woman—*alive*'.

Part 5

Suggestions for further reading

The text

Page references in these Notes are to the Penguin edition:
LAWRENCE, D.H.: *Women in Love*, Penguin Books (in association with William Heinemann), Harmondsworth, 1977. *Women in Love* was first published in London by Martin Secker in 1921; the novel was first published by William Heinemann in 1954; first published by Penguin in 1960.

Other works by D.H. Lawrence

Lawrence wrote over fifty books. Most are available in hardback, published by Heinemann, London, and in paperback, published by Penguin Books, Harmondsworth.

The following titles (all in Penguin editions) are recommended for beginners:
The White Peacock, 1911
Sons and Lovers, 1913
The Rainbow, 1915
Twilight in Italy, 1916 (travel)
England, My England, 1922 (stories)
The Ladybird, The Fox, The Captain's Doll, 1923
St Mawr, 1925
Lady Chatterley's Lover, Florence, 1928; London, 1960
The Virgin and the Gypsy, 1930
Phoenix: The Posthumous Papers, edited by Edward D. McDonald, 1936
Selected Letters, edited by Richard Aldington, 1950
Phoenix II: Uncollected, Unpublished and Other Prose Works, edited by Warren Roberts and Harry T. Moore, 1968. Includes Lawrence's 'Foreword to *Women in Love*' and 'Prologue' to *Women in Love*
The Complete Poems, edited by Vivian de Sola Pinto and Warren Roberts, 1964

Biography

MOORE, HARRY T.: *The Priest of Love: A Life of D.H. Lawrence*, revised edition, Heinemann, London, 1974; Penguin Books, Harmondsworth, 1976

NEHLS, EDWARD H.: *D.H. Lawrence: A Composite Biography*, 3 vols, University of Wisconsin Press, Madison, 1957–9

SAGAR, KEITH: *The Life of D.H. Lawrence: An Illustrated Biography*, Eyre Methuen, London, 1980

Criticism

ALCORN, JOHN: *The Nature Novel from Hardy to Lawrence*, Macmillan, London, 1977

ALLDRITT, KEITH: *The Visual Imagination of D.H. Lawrence*, Edward Arnold, London, 1971

BEAL, ANTHONY: *D.H. Lawrence* (Writers and Critics Series), Oliver & Boyd, Edinburgh, 1961

CLARKE, COLIN (ed.): *The Rainbow and Women in Love: A Selection of Critical Essays* (Casebook Series), Macmillan, London, 1969

COOMBES, H. (ed.): *D.H. Lawrence: A Critical Anthology*, Penguin Books, Harmondsworth, 1973

HOUGH, GRAHAM: *The Dark Sun*, Duckworth, London, 1956

KERMODE, FRANK: *Lawrence*, Fontana Collins, London, 1973

LEAVIS, F.R.: *D.H. Lawrence: Novelist*, Chatto & Windus, London, 1955; Penguin Books, Harmondsworth, 1973

PRITCHARD, R.E.: *D.H. Lawrence: Body of Darkness*, Hutchinson, London, 1971

SAGAR, KEITH: *The Art of D.H. Lawrence*, Cambridge University Press, Cambridge, 1966

STEWART, J.I.M.: *Eight Modern Writers*, Oxford University Press, London, 1963. There is a good account of *Women in Love* in the chapter on Lawrence

TIVERTON, FATHER WILLIAM (Father Martin Jarrett-Kerr): *D.H. Lawrence and Human Experience*, Rockliff, London, 1951

WILLIAMS, RAYMOND: *The English Novel from Dickens to Lawrence*, Chatto & Windus, London, 1970; Paladin, St Albans, 1974

YOUNG, KENNETH: *D.H. Lawrence* (Writers and their Work), Longman, for the British Council, Harlow, 1952, 1969

The author of these notes

NEIL MCEWAN was educated at Pembroke College, Oxford. He has taught at universities in England, Canada and Africa, and is at present Lecturer in English at the University of Qatar. He has written the York Notes on L.P. Hartley's *The Go-Between*; Henry James's *Daisy Miller* and *The Europeans;* Evelyn Waugh's *Decline and Fall*; and the York Handbooks *Preparing for Examinations in English Literature* and *Style in English Prose*. He is the author of *The Survival of the Novel* (Macmillan) and *Africa and the Novel* (Macmillan).

York Notes: list of titles

CHINUA ACHEBE
Things Fall Apart

EDWARD ALBEE
Who's Afraid of Virginia Woolf?

MARGARET ATWOOD
The Handmaid's Tale

W. H. AUDEN
Selected Poems

JANE AUSTEN
Emma
Mansfield Park
Northanger Abbey
Persuasion
Pride and Prejudice
Sense and Sensibility

SAMUEL BECKETT
Waiting for Godot

ARNOLD BENNETT
The Card

JOHN BETJEMAN
Selected Poems

WILLIAM BLAKE
Songs of Innocence, Songs of Experience

ROBERT BOLT
A Man For All Seasons

CHARLOTTE BRONTË
Jane Eyre

EMILY BRONTË
Wuthering Heights

BYRON
Selected Poems

GEOFFREY CHAUCER
The Clerk's Tale
The Franklin's Tale
The Knight's Tale
The Merchant's Tale
The Miller's Tale
The Nun's Priest's Tale
The Pardoner's Tale
Prologue to the Canterbury Tales
The Wife of Bath's Tale

SAMUEL TAYLOR COLERIDGE
Selected Poems

JOSEPH CONRAD
Heart of Darkness

DANIEL DEFOE
Moll Flanders
Robinson Crusoe

SHELAGH DELANEY
A Taste of Honey

CHARLES DICKENS
Bleak House
David Copperfield
Great Expectations
Hard Times
Oliver Twist

EMILY DICKINSON
Selected Poems

JOHN DONNE
Selected Poems

DOUGLAS DUNN
Selected Poems

GERALD DURRELL
My Family and Other Animals

GEORGE ELIOT
Middlemarch
The Mill on the Floss
Silas Marner

T. S. ELIOT
Four Quartets
Murder in the Cathedral
Selected Poems
The Waste Land

WILLIAM FAULKNER
The Sound and the Fury

HENRY FIELDING
Joseph Andrews
Tom Jones

F. SCOTT FITZGERALD
The Great Gatsby
Tender is the Night

GUSTAVE FLAUBERT
Madame Bovary

E. M. FORSTER
Howards End
A Passage to India

JOHN FOWLES
The French Lieutenant's Woman

ELIZABETH GASKELL
North and South

WILLIAM GOLDING
Lord of the Flies

GRAHAM GREENE
Brighton Rock
The Heart of the Matter
The Power and the Glory

THOMAS HARDY
Far from the Madding Crowd
Jude the Obscure
The Mayor of Casterbridge
The Return of the Native
Selected Poems
Tess of the D'Urbervilles

L. P. HARTLEY
The Go-Between

NATHANIEL HAWTHORNE
The Scarlet Letter

SEAMUS HEANEY
Selected Poems

ERNEST HEMINGWAY
A Farewell to Arms
The Old Man and the Sea

SUSAN HILL
I'm the King of the Castle

HOMER
The Iliad
The Odyssey

GERARD MANLEY HOPKINS
Selected Poems

TED HUGHES
Selected Poems

ALDOUS HUXLEY
Brave New World

HENRY JAMES
The Portrait of a Lady

BEN JONSON
The Alchemist
Volpone

JAMES JOYCE
Dubliners
A Portrait of the Artist as a Young Man

JOHN KEATS
Selected Poems

PHILIP LARKIN
Selected Poems

D. H. LAWRENCE
The Rainbow
Selected Short Stories
Sons and Lovers
Women in Love

HARPER LEE
To Kill a Mockingbird

LAURIE LEE
Cider with Rosie

CHRISTOPHER MARLOWE
Doctor Faustus

ARTHUR MILLER
The Crucible
Death of a Salesman
A View from the Bridge

JOHN MILTON
Paradise Lost I & II
Paradise Lost IV & IX

SEAN O'CASEY
Juno and the Paycock

GEORGE ORWELL
Animal Farm
Nineteen Eighty-four

JOHN OSBORNE
Look Back in Anger

WILFRED OWEN
Selected Poems

HAROLD PINTER
The Caretaker

SYLVIA PLATH
Selected Works

ALEXANDER POPE
Selected Poems

J. B. PRIESTLEY
An Inspector Calls

WILLIAM SHAKESPEARE
Antony and Cleopatra
As You Like It
Coriolanus
Hamlet
Henry IV Part I
Henry IV Part II
Henry V
Julius Caesar
King Lear
Macbeth
Measure for Measure
The Merchant of Venice
A Midsummer Night's Dream
Much Ado About Nothing
Othello
Richard II
Richard III
Romeo and Juliet
Sonnets
The Taming of the Shrew
The Tempest

Troilus and Cressida
Twelfth Night
The Winter's Tale

GEORGE BERNARD SHAW
Arms and the Man
Pygmalion
Saint Joan

MARY SHELLEY
Frankenstein

PERCY BYSSHE SHELLEY
Selected Poems

RICHARD BRINSLEY SHERIDAN
The Rivals

R. C. SHERRIFF
Journey's End

JOHN STEINBECK
The Grapes of Wrath
Of Mice and Men
The Pearl

TOM STOPPARD
Rosencrantz and Guildenstern are Dead

JONATHAN SWIFT
Gulliver's Travels

JOHN MILLINGTON SYNGE
The Playboy of the Western World

W. M. THACKERAY
Vanity Fair

MARK TWAIN
Huckleberry Finn

VIRGIL
The Aeneid

DEREK WALCOTT
Selected Poems

ALICE WALKER
The Color Purple

JOHN WEBSTER
The Duchess of Malfi

OSCAR WILDE
The Importance of Being Earnest

THORNTON WILDER
Our Town

TENNESSEE WILLIAMS
The Glass Menagerie

VIRGINIA WOOLF
Mrs Dalloway
To the Lighthouse

WILLIAM WORDSWORTH
Selected Poems

W. B. YEATS
Selected Poems